RICHARD M PEARSON

DEADWATER

First Edition

Cover design & Typesetting by Ryan Ashcroft

Dedicated to my Soulmate

Contents

It is only when you look back at things from the distance of many years that you finally understand why. The problem was we in the village blamed the aristocratic Denham-Granger family for our bad fortune. Everything was their fault according to us but in hindsight, that was more to do with jealousy than reality. We hated them because they had wealth and looked down on us as uneducated peasants. But the truth was, they were as much victims as we were. No, the real holder of all the power through the years was Deadwater. The grand three-story country mansion cast its shadow over the village and manipulated everything to survive. So, when it realised that time was running out it played the final card, and then dark retribution crawled out of that room to hunt each of its victims down.

Thoughts:

The very moment you read the first word of the opening chapter, the clock will start ticking and your destiny will forever be entwined with my story. Is that not why we are all here, hoping to escape the shadow cast by Deadwater House?

1

SKELETON KEYS

(Deadwater House 1984)

I stood on the steps and watched the last occupant of Deadwater House being carried into the back of the ambulance. Even as they closed the doors it was still possible to hear the spiteful shrieking of the man I had known for the last eight years as John Denham-Granger. The man who had tormented me throughout my time as the Witton Saint James police constable. The man who had finally destroyed my career with his evil hatred of me and every other villager. I waited until the ambulance disappeared behind the overgrown trees and bushes of the ruined garden before turning to face the imposing three-story mansion.

So, this was it, fate had played the final card and for once it had fallen in my favour. The hopeless policeman who had failed to find out the truth of what was hidden inside those fading walls. Years of gossip and rumour, years of finger pointing and blame. And now finally I was alone at Deadwater Mansion. At long last, I could climb the stairs to the little back room with the window and find out the truth. No more would John Denham-Granger mock and taunt me while his beloved wife Roberta stood in the shadows behind him. The last two heirs of Deadwater House had gone and finally, the crumbling building would be forced to give up its terrible secret.

I edged quietly through what had once been considered a classic stately home. Old newspapers and discarded rubbish strewn across the floors. A film of grime covered the glass of the large ornate windows. The all-pervading smell of damp invaded my nostrils as I started the climb to the third floor. Utter silence only broken by the sound of the grand staircase groaning in protest at the unwanted intruder. I had no right to be here, I was no longer even an acting policeman. But I could sense the eyes of the village watching and waiting. Don't screw up this time Gordon, you owe us. This all started the day you arrived as our new constable. Don't you dare run away and leave the ghost of Deadwater to continue its curse? Since the apparition appeared it had impacted on us all including the occupants of Deadwater house. They had suffered more than anyone, but I felt no sympathy for John Denham-Granger and his darling

Roberta. They could have ended my misery, they could have cleared it all up years ago, but they chose not to. Had it all just been to enjoy a long drawn out revenge on the village, on me, and now came the punch-line? Behind that door, in that room lay the answer. The answer to the masterful joke they had played on us all.

I took the last few steps towards the large steel door that had been locked for so many years and I prayed, prayed that we had all been wrong. Prayed that I had not failed in my job and the deaths had all been a coincidence. Prayed that we had all been the victims of mass hysteria fuelled by narrow-minded villager's intent on blaming the Denham-Grangers for everything. And I whispered beneath my breath in that dark hallway as I reached the room, the room that had invaded my dreams for so long, I whispered, Oh God please do not let me find the long-decayed body of the fabled Denham-Granger child hidden behind this door.

Thoughts:

I tend to think that colour was only invented the day I was born. It must be because the only reference I have of the time before then is old black and white movies and photographs. The men all wore hats, it made them look old, even the young ones. The women covered their legs in long dresses but even though they looked poor they somehow seemed sophisticated. Until they spoke that is, then it was all cockney accents and cigarettes hanging from the corner of their mouths. You could always hear train whistles in the distance but would never see a train. Smoke, soot and dim lights shining on the cobbled streets.

2

I SEE YOU

(Witton Saint James 1976)

Robbie sat at the edge of the stream watching the still pool of water. The baking summer had long ago dried up the flow and now instead of the familiar shaded wood and milling tadpoles, he had the stagnant water and endless midges to keep him company. He waited for his two friends Carl and Steven with a growing sense of nervousness and anticipation. It was not trespassing up at Deadwater House than concerned him, it was the ridicule he would have to face from his accomplices if the boy in the window did not reappear. Robbie was convinced he had seen him, a pale white shadow staring down on that late summer afternoon a few days before. He had already filled his bag with fallen apples from the side of the house when something made him turn back and look. At

least twenty panes of dark glass on three levels
reflected the descending sun but one of them, the
small top floor window was open even though like all
the rear windows of the house it was encased with
iron bars. It looked like a boy, the apparition hardly
moved. At that distance, it could have been anything
but since the sighting, Robbie's imagination had set
the image in stone, a boy it had to be. And then the
vision had been romantically embellished over the
following days, now it was a child who was being held
captive by the strange Denham-Grangers. He was
desperate to escape but the window was too high
from the ground, only they could rescue him.

Robbie stirred out of his daydreaming as he heard
the others scrambling up the side of the little forest.
He could make out the voices of Carl and Steven, but
the other sound was less familiar. With a growing
sense of resentment, he knew it had to be Imelda, *that
idiot Carl had brought her along, again. Why would anyone
bring a girl on such an important mission*? And yet, even
Robbie half understood the changes that he was going
through, fourteen was no longer a child but it was
nowhere near an adult. He knew the real reason he
did not want Imelda along, he was jealous of Carl, he
wanted a girlfriend as well and he wished it was
Imelda.

'Captain Robbie, all present and correct sir,'
shouted Carl while giving a mock salute.

It was hard to be annoyed with the already tall and

handsome Carl, he was the one they should really be saluting. He and Robbie had been village friends since the start of primary school while Steven had not arrived on the scene until a few years later. Playground Hierarchy would forever deem the pecking order of the three friends to always leave Steven as the newcomer.

'Ooh, I did not realise you had been promoted to a Captain, Robbie. I thought you had to be more than three feet tall for that job?'

Even at the age of fourteen Imelda could tease the boys and they would accept it. Robbie turned quickly before anyone would notice him blush, but Imelda smiled to herself, she understood already.

'Right, let's stop fucking around, be as quiet as possible, follow me,' Robbie shouted before heading through the wood towards the imposing mansion of Deadwater. Carl and Imelda tried not to laugh at the officious tone that Robbie had adopted.

The four friends crept quietly towards the edge of the small wood that kept them concealed at the rear of the imposing building. There was still at least three hundred yards to cover through the open lawn and scattered apple trees. The group banked on the two occupants of the house being either out or engaged in some task that would not require them to look out of the rear windows. Robbie felt confident they would not be seen, he had been here many times to collect apples and had never encountered the Denham-Grangers or anyone else for that matter. Well not until the face at the window had appeared.

'Ok Captain Robbie, what window is it and where is our friend the boy ghost?' Imelda chuckled at Carl's mocking tone.

'We need to get up beside the back of the house, keep near the apple trees and don't make any noise.' Robbie's words came out with surprising authority as he tried to ignore the jibes. They followed his instructions until the group all stood at the back of the house directly underneath the second-floor window that was the object of their mission.

'Hello, Heellooo,' Robbie had barely let out the words directed at the glass forty feet above him when Carl and Imelda broke into fits of giggling. Only Steven remained silent, while Robbie felt his face redden with anger.

'Look, if you two don't want to take this seriously then fuck off back home.' Carl looked at his friend and shrugged.

'This is daft Robbie, there is no one here except the Denham-Grangers, why don't we head back to the village, this is boring.'

But Robbie had no choice now, he had to follow the mission through or face being made to look like a child in front of Imelda. Carl and the girl wandered off back into the cover of the apple trees and lay down some distance away to enjoy the sun and laugh at the two boys.

'What shall we do then Robbie, I don't see anyone up at the window?' Steven eyed up his friend while waiting for his instruction on what the next step would be. When Robbie did not reply Steven started walking off towards the dilapidated garden sheds that bordered the edge of the house.

'Wait for me.' Robbie ran off to catch up with him. Somehow, he had a feeling this might not end well.

Carl and Imelda watched from the cover of the trees with growing disbelief as the two distant boys re-appeared from one of the decrepit outhouses with an old wooden ladder. Already they knew the escapade was going too far and would lead to trouble. Imelda took Carl's arm and pulled him towards the forest that bordered the property. 'Carl, I don't like this, we are going to get into big trouble. If we get caught my mum will kill me. Let's get out of here, please.'

Even though they wanted to get away, the fascination of what would happen next held them both entranced. They walked back to the forest to give them enough distance to escape but close enough to just make out what was happening.

Underneath the window, Robbie and Steven positioned the ancient ladder. Once extended to its full length it was just tall enough to reach a few feet below the small upper floor window. Robbie tried not to show that he was frightened, and that Steven had taken control. This had happened in the past, most recently when his friend had got carried away when they had used their air guns on the village cats. Something about Steven always made him push things too far and now Robbie could not back out as he knew Imelda would be watching from the trees. 'I will climb up, you hold the ladder,' Robbie whispered to his accomplice.

'No, I am going, it was my idea to get the ladder,' retorted Steven.

'I am fucking doing it, hold the fucking ladder and do as I say.'

Robbie's stern reply was enough to put Steven back in his place and he took up position, holding the ladder with a remorseful look almost as though he was going to cry. Looking back on this day some years later Robbie would still feel a pang of guilt. It would take the maturity of adulthood for him to understand the pattern of Steven's behaviour that would see his friend dead before he left his teens.

Robbie was nearing the last rungs and was now only a few feet short of the small barred window. From ground level it did not look too high, from the top of the old wooden ladder it seemed terrifyingly far above the ground. He had already made his mind up, he would reach the window, push it open through the bars, pretend he was speaking to someone and then get the hell away from Deadwater House. Whether Carl and Imelda believed him or not about the imprisoned boy no longer mattered, he had gone as far as he could. Robbie reached the top of the ladder and stretched his arms out to hold onto the bars of the little window. His eye level was just enough to peer into the filthy glass and freeing up one unsteady hand he pushed the frame inwards. The glare of the sun made it difficult to see inside but the smell that seeped out of the opening was enough to make Robbie retch. Whatever was in the room was either dead and decaying or maybe it was being used to store rotting food. 'Is there anyone inside, hello, anyone in there?' He felt ridiculous and wanted desperately to end the charade and climb down.

The hand and arm that grabbed Robbie from the inside would be something that would forever haunt his nightmares, but it would be the words, pathetic pleading words that filtered out of the room that would invade his thoughts every waking day. 'Water, water, please, oh God please get me water.' The sound was barely a whisper, as though whoever it was or whatever it was had uttered their final sentence. The skeletal hand and arm that tried to hold him from inside the window looked as if it had crept out of a grave. Even as the words came out Robbie was already sliding, stumbling, clawing his way down as fast as was humanly possible. Ten feet from the ground he lost control completely and crashed onto the lawn. Despite hitting the grass hard and being winded Robbie was already aware of the large figure of John Denham-Granger bearing down on him across the garden,

'You fucking little bastards, how dare you invade my property. You will pay for this you village scumbags'

But Robbie had no intention of paying for anything and despite the hard landing he was already on his feet and running, running as though his life depended on it. Running after the already fleeing Steven and the distant giggling Carl and Imelda who had taken flight as soon as the hulk of the rotund homeowner appeared at the back of the house. Denham-Granger made a grab for Robbie as the boy started to accelerate away. His fingers just caught the arm of his jacket ripping into his flesh, but the older man was already out of breath and had lost the chase.

'Run you little fuckers, that's it run back to the rest of the rats in the village. One day I will make you all pay.'

Within minutes the youngsters had left the sight of Deadwater to arrive hidden, deep in the little forest. Robbie came last crashing through the trees, Carl and Imelda lay laughing hysterically together while Steven was doubled up trying to catch his breath. Robbie already knew that they had only run because of Denham-Granger and the story of the arm in the window would be ridiculed. But that was not why he carried on fleeing past them and not stopping until he reached the village and the safety of his house. No, the reason he did not wait was the shame of letting Imelda and his friends know that he had wet himself in terror and he would continue to do so for many years after. When the memory of that voice and the smell of death came each night through the black darkness to haunt him.

Imelda watched Robbie disappear into the trees. The other two boys were still laughing from the adrenalin rush of the chase but somehow her female intuition warned her that something had happened. 'Carl for Christ sake will you stop laughing. What is up with Robbie, why did he not stop?'

'I don't know Imelda, I am sure he will be fine. Let's get out of here before Denham-Granger sets his dogs on us.'

The three friends wandered back down the forest track in the same direction that Robbie had gone. The boys chatted and laughed while Imelda stayed silent. Somehow, she knew that life had changed for them all that day. Little did any of them know just how much heartbreak they would suffer because of their innocent teenage escapade.

***

(Witton Saint James 1976)

I remember the day as though it was yesterday, maybe it stayed in my memory because it was so hot during that summer. I had only been in the job for a year and was still a raw village constable. The position in the hamlet of Witton Saint James suited me because it was barely 30 miles from Ludlow my hometown. My mum would drive her old car down the country roads to visit me. She would bring food parcels as she was convinced I would starve myself on the other side of the world. The tiny village police station was no bigger than a large shed, maybe I exaggerate but it was small. It had a reception desk, a little office at the back and believe it or not two tiny one-man cells. I tended to use them to store my bicycle or to get a quick nap during the afternoon to help pass the hours. I would lock up each night and walk the few hundred yards to my digs with the Whitby's, endless children and dogs but fond memories.

Roberta Denham-Granger stood at the desk looking down at me, even then I thought it was odd that her husband John had not come along himself to blame the trespassing on me. 'Look Constable Chisbold, you really ought to do something other than writing things down. We have had an utterly frightful experience. John is not well, and this sort of thing is really very distressing for the two of us.'

'It's Chisholme madam, not Chisbold.'

I tried to smile but she continued to talk as though I was one of the perpetrators of this awful crime. I suppose she was right in a way, the boys she described that her husband had seen would hardly be much younger than I was.

'I will look into this Mrs. Denham-Granger, it is not as though there are a lot of teenagers in the village, I am sure I will find the culprits and get back to you.'

Roberta looked into my eyes, 'I know you will Constable Chisbold, I know you will.'

And with a final flourish and a twirl of her summer dress, she walked out of the police shed and into her bright yellow Cortina. Even in her early fifties Roberta was a striking looking woman and carried herself as though she owned the world, and of course, to the village she did. Maybe the Denham-Grangers did not have much money, drive a Rolls Royce or have servants. They owned Deadwater House and to the inhabitants of Witton St James, that made them royalty.

A few hours later I closed the police station for the evening and decided to take in a visit to The Oak. The village pub was my best hope of getting some information on the supposed house breakers of

Deadwater. Even then it seemed obvious to me that the culprits were no worse than a few bored teenagers, but I also knew I would have to report something back to the Denham-Grangers. I pushed the door of The Oak open and walked into the bar. The faces of the all-male population turned around to see who the new arrival would be.

'You old enough to drink in ere then Gordon?' I knew my appearance in uniform would start the wisecracks, but I accepted it came with the territory.

'Ahh Mister Davington, I thought I would find you in your usual seat, maybe you could help me out?'

Of course, each village pub has its gossip sitting at the corner of the bar listening to everyone else's business and Farmer Paul Davington was a master at it. As usual, he held sway with the other men dotted along the bar. Even in the mid-seventies the village pub was a male stronghold and equality was still some years away, or at least that's how I remember it. Men came to drink to forget about their wives and children. It was easier to hide in those days as well, no mobile phones and if the misses called the pub landline then either the landlord or the customers would lie for you. *Arthur, no I have not seen him. He has not been in all day. Yes of course, if he does appear we will tell him to come home immediately as his dinner is in the oven. Ok cheerio.* The phone would go down and then Arthur would go up to the bar to buy another round.

'You in ere to find out what appened at the big ouse then?

I should have known that the grapevine would carry any unusual happening in the village at the speed of light.

'Yes, Mister Davington, you heard anything?'

'Only a rumour ah hurd bout them boys what went up to the big ouse lookin for the face in the winder.'

'Who were the boys then?' I asked the question knowing full well that Davington was a gossip not a grass and the names even if he knew them would not be divulged. Even more so to me a village outsider.

'Don't know of none boys but I does know that them Denham-Grangers are a strange lot. Paid off the gardner and the last ouskeeper, runs out of money I reckons. No surprise once the father died and that useless waster of a son John took over, an that hoity-toity wuman Roberta what tells him what to do anyways. Should a been Arry what took over, he was the clever wun.'

Old Farmer Davington was away on one of his never-ending rants, I cut in quickly.

'You mentioned a face in the window Mister Davington, what's that all about?'

'I urd they keepin their child locked away in the winder room cos they shamed ee is deformed. Not goin to suit er ighness Lady Roberta to ave a deformed child messin up er place. Be what I urd and be the truth no doubt'

And that was the first time I heard the rumour, the same one that would follow in my shadow every day for the next 8 years as the Witton St James police constable. I suppose as the years went by I started to believe it myself. But one thing was for sure, no way was I going to start poking about Deadwater House. Television detectives solved mysteries like that, not village constables. Anyway, just like the rest of them, I might talk behind the Denham-Grangers back, but I would still doff my hat to their faces.

As I walked up to my digs at the Whitby's I tried to put Famer Davington's usual rumour and gossip into perspective. I knew the names of the teenage culprits would never be handed over to me, a new constable barely in my twenties as well as an outsider from the other side of the world, 30 miles away. The villagers could gossip until the cows came home but when it came to their own folk, they would close ranks. In their eyes the problem was not the teenagers it was the Denham-Grangers, or should I say the current Denham-Grangers. The old master of Deadwater, Leonard Denham-Granger had at least been respected from a distance if not liked. His heir John was mostly ignored at that time, and the vitriol directed at his wife Roberta, the interloper from London. I had already decided it was not worth wasting time trying to track down the two boys they had reported as running away. Farmer Davington would spread the word that whoever it was would be in serious trouble, that would be enough to frighten off any further intruders. I could then visit Deadwater house and hopefully spin John Denham-Granger a yarn to fob him off and just hope Roberta was out for the day.

Approaching the gate into the little terraced Whitby house I stopped for a few seconds to think about the face in the window story. Of course, I knew it was just that, the whimsical imagination of bored summer teenagers. The idea of an imprisoned child was ridiculous and yet, something did not seem right. On the advice of Sergeant Lawson in Ludlow, I had taken the time during my first year to get to talk to everyone in the village, let them know I was a friendly face. Most had been ok if slightly standoffish, some had been downright condescending. They had been comfortable with old PC Thrower, he had just been a walking talking gossip machine, so, he fitted in perfectly. I doubted he had ever done any real police work in all his years in the village and now with my patch starting change was in the air. Now even the village bobby had to justify his existence, show he was doing something for his £65 a week. In my first few days, I went up to Deadwater to introduce myself and found John Denham-Granger to be the easiest going and most helpful person in the village. How ironic that he was so laid back and open. I wondered whether he was drunk or maybe smoked marijuana, the house had a strange smell. At the time and being so naive I put it down to the place being old and damp. Roberta had wandered in and given a courteous hello before quickly disappearing.

'So, do you have many staff here these days Mr. Denham-Granger?'

It was a stupid question I know but I was searching desperately for something to say. Would you have done any better at twenty?

'No Gordon, and do please call me John, young man, Mister-Denham Granger sounds positively Orwellian. Money is tight these days, just enough to keep us in gin.' He winked and gave me a smile.

'Just the housekeeper and gardener, both finished and away for the day young sir. Just me and the lady in the house, suits me fine young chap.'

To me on that first visit in 1975 it seemed friendly and easy going in the supposed house of evil that the villagers regarded with disdain from a distance. I remember standing up to leave and John grasping my hand and shaking it as though I was a long-lost cousin. Through the large living room window, I could make out the not unpleasant figure of Roberta bending down to pick flowers from the well-tended garden beds.

One of the Whitby dogs roared up to the gate and suddenly shook me out of my thoughts. Mrs. Whitby heard the commotion and leaned out of the window of the little house,

'Hurry up Gordon, I have a lovely pot of Vegetable and Ham soup on the boil here.'

I smiled and walked up to the door. But I still had time for one more memory of my first visit to Deadwater. As I got onto my Police issue bicycle that day something made me turn around and look up at the front of the house. John still stood in the doorway watching me leave and Roberta remained engrossed in the garden. Or was it all just a big act, an attempt to show that everything was normal? Whoever observed from one of the upper floor windows did not expect me to look back, and the curtain was quickly pulled over to cover the glass. At the time it did seem odd as John Denham-Granger had made it quite clear that only him and his wife were in the house. In fact, he had pushed the point that they were alone. But whoever was with them was certainly not being held captive or surely, they would have shouted or done something to attract my attention. And who was I to dare question the Denham-Grangers anyway? they were village royalty after all. As I mentioned, there to be talked about behind their backs but never to be challenged.

Thoughts:

My first real memory would be around the age of two when my mum pushed me in a pram across a busy London street. I vaguely remember being fascinated by one of those red and white poles spinning around outside a barber's shop. I suppose we must have been easily impressed in those days. Even at that age I hated being confined. My mother would only have been a kid herself and I was convinced she was going to get both of us killed as she manoeuvred the pushchair around the cars. I suppose it was an early case of me being a back-seat driver.

3

YESTERDAY'S CHILD

(Deadwater House 1950)

Old man Leonard Denham-Granger's face boiled as if it had been dunked in scalding water. The veins on his neck stood out in anger as he faced up to his youngest son Harry, 'You leave this time and I swear to God Harry I am finished with you, no going back, no money, nothing. You walk out, and the door is shut forever. No inheritance, no allowance. I am damned if I will put up with your resentment any longer. You have threatened me one last time son, this time I mean it.'

Harry stared back at him, a portrait of barely suppressed bitterness and rage. He may have only been 22 but he was taller and stronger than the old man. This gave him the physical advantage over his father, but money always beat everything in the poker game of life. The old man used it to control the errant Harry and his older brother John. 'It's not your fucking money dad, it belonged to mum as well.'

'Your mother is dead Harry, dead, she is no longer here to make excuses for you every time you throw a tantrum. When the hell are you ever going to accept that fact and grow up.'

John as always stood on the sidelines watching like a referee during a boxing match. He had seen all this before, but he sensed that this time it would be different. His younger brother had built up the resentment all his life and now the volcano was ready to erupt.

'Maybe mum would still be here if you had left her alone you fucking big bully.' Harry was shaking with anger now as he screamed at his father. John as ever the pacifier tried to intervene.

'I say chaps, maybe we should calm down a bit. All this shouting is not going to help anyone.'

'Shut up John, this has nothing to do with you.' Leonard barked the words out at the older boy before moving within inches of Harry's face. He stared unblinkingly into his young son's eyes before uttering the final words of the argument.

'Your mother spoiled you, Harry, she always did. You are still like an angry child, crying for his mummy to come and spoon feed him.'

He spat out the words with venom but even as he finished the sentence he knew it had been the wrong thing to say and at exactly the wrong time. Harry finally cracked, always on a short leash and liable to lash out, the arguments had never gone as far as physical violence…until now. The blow sent old Leonard Denham-Granger staggering backwards, almost in slow motion. Then his body finally accepted it had been hit with full force and he crashed over the oak table and landed with a sickening thud onto the large woven rug.

John sat on the wall that edged up to the small wood bordering Deadwater House. He looked at his younger brother with a feeling of sadness. It was not that the two of them were particularly close. The four-year age difference seemed to separate them almost the way the wall kept the big house and the distant village apart. John now knew that Harry would have no choice but to leave and probably for good. That meant the older boy would be forced to take over the business when the old man passed away. John dreaded the thought of following in his father's footsteps, he had no desire to sit at a desk all day dealing with the workers, finances and everything else involved in running a large company. He had always hoped that Harry would eventually grow up and take over, leaving him to enjoy his share of the money without having to do any real graft. 'Is the old bastard going to be ok?' Harry asked the question with a resigned tone, almost as though he no longer cared what his future held.

'He will be ok, I think you hurt dad's pride more than anything. It was a fair punch old chap, maybe a bit over the top all the same.' John spoke the words in the same calm tone that he used for every situation.

'Bloody hell John does nothing ever get you annoyed? I wish to God I could be more like you. The old git just gets me so angry. He destroyed mum with his temper, she would still be here today if it was not for that old bastard.' Deborah Denham Granger had died 10 years before in 1940, she was still relatively young, and it had impacted the then 12-year-old Harry far more than the four years older John.

'To be honest old chap, I am not sure it is fair to blame the old man for everything, mum never kept the best of health. Ok maybe he could have been easier on her at times, but, well you know...' Harry turned to look at his brother incredulously, with rising anger in his voice.

'That's your bloody trouble John, everything goes over your head. For Christ sake I am not saying he killed her, I am just saying he bullied her, never gave her any credit, treated her as though he owned her the same as that bloody business he loves so much.' John tried to steer the conversation back to the present, the last thing he needed was to rile his loose tempered brother any more than he already was.

'So, what are you going to do Harry, old chap?'

'Got no bloody choice now have I. Might as well take up that offer in the Merchant Navy that I told you about. Get away from him and this house. Did you get the money from my room you went to find?' John fumbled in his pocket and handed his young brother the envelope.

'I found your £500 and added in another £200 I have been saving as well.' Even this last act of kindness could not bring the brothers any closer, 22 years of indifference and occasional animosity on Harry's part could not be fixed with £200. Harry jumped off the wall and turned to shake John's hand, a last formal act before they would part.

'Take care old chap, maybe one day you will come back eh? Save me having to run the business when the old man gives it up?' But John knew that Harry would not be back anytime soon, the end had come the second he pulled his arm back and landed the blow on the old man's head. Harry looked at his older brother and winked.

'I will be back the day that old bastard dies. You can run the fucking business if you want, just make sure you keep my half of the cash.'

And then without another word Harry walked off through the woods towards the village. The £700 was a lot of money at the start of the austere fifties. It would keep Harry in relative luxury until he got to sign on and sail the high seas as far away from Deadwater as possible. And that was the last time John would see or even hear from his firebrand brother for almost 24 years.

Old Denham-Granger dabbed the handkerchief on his swollen lip and winced in pain. Maud the housekeeper had been insistent that she send for the local doctor, but Leonard would have none of it. If the village got to hear of the family coming to blows the name Denham-Granger would be disgraced and the old man could not live with that. And yet for all that his head and back hurt it could not match the pain in his heart. The pain of now having to accept that he had gone too far and pushed Harry to the limit. *Why could he never hold back and give the boy a chance?* But that was old Denham-Grangers problem. He ran everything including his family as though it was a business and harsh cutting words were all that would be needed to make everyone jump to his command. And now he was left with the nightmare he had dreaded. He knew that Harry was like him, angry with the world and ready to take on every challenge. *The younger son would have finally grown up and taken over, but he had ruined it, pushed him too far.* So, he was left with John. How could two boys that looked so much like each other be so different? Leonard knew that his empire would crumble if John was left to look after things. Within months, weeks even, the business would collapse around the elder boy as he looked to others to make decisions. That had always been the issue for the old man. In his own way, he loved Harry, but he was indifferent to the older boy. He even wondered at times if John's almost feminine easy-going nature meant he was queer, a poof, certainly not a man who could be relied on to drive a business. *No bloody backbone John, that has always been your problem. You should have been a bloody girl.* But the reality was, John was all the old man had left now, whether he liked it or not.

So, the three men each walked off in different directions on that balmy early evening in late 1950. One heading away to his new life, one walking back with dread to face the changes in his life and one paced the floor of the house and worried about the future. But the thing that did not change was Deadwater House, it stood tall and proud as always and still held the real power of the Denham-Granger family.

***

(Witton Saint James 1978)

It's odd looking back on my career as the Witton Saint James Policeman or Bobby as they used to call us. After all this time my memories seem to collide into each other and become a dull mix of forgotten incidents and routine. I don't know why but I seem to remember times better when they are related to Deadwater house or if I am honest, the hidden child and well, that thing. It would be 1978 that would next stick in my mind, for two reasons.

The first was the party. By this time, I had moved into my own small village house, well you could hardly call it a house. It was just a tiny cottage on the very edge of Witton Saint James. Two rooms, one to eat and sit in and one to sleep in. The toilet was outside in a lean-to building. The only heating came from the living room fireplace that I rarely lit. I suppose being only 22 the cold did not impact me and like all young men, I was too lazy to make a fire anyway. Eventually, I think my mother bought me an electric fire after she had visited one day and nearly died of hypothermia. Each evening after I had closed the tiny police station and stored away my bike I would head to the fish and chip shop. The seventies did not have such a hang-up about health foods so that was my staple diet pretty much every day. Well, all the gym worshippers and vegetable eaters may well frown, but I am still here while many others in my story seem to have already passed to the other side.

So, the party. I had finished my fish and chips, messed about with that hopeless little tv for a while trying to get a signal and finally retired to bed. It was Friday and my mum was coming over to pick me up in the morning. Her plan was to take me back to Ludlow for the weekend to feed me up, so I would not die of self-inflicted starvation for another few weeks at least. I would normally have gone to The Oak for a couple of pints on the last day of the week but had decided to keep a clear head for the morning, a good decision as it turned out. It must have been around midnight when I was woken by the phone ringing in the living room. Of course, it had to be police business, who the hell else would call me at that hour? I reckon it was only the second time the phone had ever rung so late during my first three years on the village beat. The other time had been kids messing around, they called me a cock and hung up.

'Hello Gordon Chisholme, speaking'

'Is that the police station, are you the policeman?' I knew straight away that it was Old Ma Capley from Daisey cottage, she had been into my police shed on several occasions, always complaining about something. To be honest she was a complete pain in the arse. She wore a hearing aid, but God knows why as she never listened to anybody.

'Yes Mrs. Capley, how are you? It's me Gordon and yes as far as I remember I am indeed the policeman. How may I help you?'

'I want the police, is that the police station?'

'Yes, yes Mrs. Capley. It's me, Gordon, you have

spoken to me many times. Gordon, Gordon, the chap who wears a police uniform when you make one of your regular visits to the police station.'

'I am looking for the police, are you the police. I want the police station?

'This is the fuc... the police station Mrs. Capley, that's how you ended up talking to me. You called here, so you must know it's the police station or you would not have called. How can I help you?'. She always riled me, I was sure the old bat did it for her own enjoyment.

'I need the police, this is an emergency I tell you. Are you the police station?'

I took a deep breath and waited until she got fed up trying to annoy me and eventually got to the real reason for her call. There followed a long drawn out and repeated story about a teenage party in number 12 three doors down from hers. The way she described it sounded like a hoard of hells angels had descended on Witton Saint James bringing death, destruction, and drugs. I got dressed wearily while wishing it really was a wild party and I could to join in. Somehow, I knew damn well it would be a handful of youngsters playing records and old Capley would still have her hearing aid switched to the maximum. Funny how she could hear a party three doors away but not listen to a word anyone said.

But for once village life would prove me wrong,

As I walked up to the front of number 12 I could hear very loud music as well as excited shouting from what was obviously a large gathering. The Warton's lived at the house with their son Steven. He was an odd little bugger, I disliked him as he showed scant respect for me as a policeman. I was sure it was him who had phoned to call me a cock and then hung up. Often while out on the beat I would hear him make loud snide remarks as I walked past, trying to impress his other teenage friends. I walked up to the open front door past young couples making out in the garden and underage drinkers swigging cans of cheap beer. Young Robbie appeared at the door. 'Hey Gordon man, how you keeping man? You come to join the party? Can I get you a beer?' He was well gone but his tone was good-natured at least.

'Is Steven here? Can you tell him I need to speak to him? I take it his parents are away?' Robbie shouted for his friend who staggered up to the door. He was holding a joint in one hand and a can of lager in the other, blatantly showing off to belittle me.

'What the fuck are you wanting then Mister Sherriff, you got your six guns with you?'

'Steven, I take it your parents are away? You need to call it a night, it's one in the morning and the noise is getting out of hand. I take it you are aware that it is illegal to smoke drugs and you also need to be eighteen to drink for that matter.' The little prick eyed me up, too drunk and too young to say anything clever, so instead I got,

'You think you are so tough Mister copper, why don't you fuck off back to finding lost cats and go pester the rest of the village?'

One of the few advantages of being a village policeman in the seventies was, in general people still held some respect for a uniform. You could get away with a lot of things in those pre-CCTV and camera phone days. I grabbed the obnoxious little runt by the scruff of his neck,

'Well, why don't we just go down to Mister Sherriff's office and you can spend the night in my little cell until I call your parents in the morning.'

I think I must have still been annoyed at old Capley waking me up as I grabbed Steven by the back of his shirt collar and started to march him down the garden path. The response was not what I had expected from the supposed tough guy as even before I got to the end of the garden Steven was crying. Someone tapped me on the shoulder, I turned around and that was the first time I remember seeing her. Well maybe not the first time but certainly the first time I had noticed her. Imelda held my arm,

'Gordon, please let him go. Steven is drunk, he does not mean anything. I will get Carl and Robbie to get him to his bed and get rid of everyone. Things just got a little out of hand, I promise we will close the party up.'

Even though she was then only sixteen Imelda spoke with the assurance of a twenty-five-year-old. She certainly looked older than her years, stunning was how I remember her. Long dark curls and blue eyes that always held an infectious smile. You must understand that in those days a 22-year-old falling in love with a sixteen-year-old was not considered out of the ordinary. Nowadays I would probably have needed to arrest myself for even considering it.

Robbie and Carl who seemed to be Imelda's boyfriend at the time got Steven up to his room. By now the beer and joint had kicked in and he could hardly walk. Not that the other two boys were much better but with my help, we started to get the rest of the teenage partygoers to clear out. God knows what Stevens parents would think when they returned from wherever they had gone. The house was a mess, drink and food crunched into the carpet, broken glass and burn marks on the furniture. It was obvious that out of towners had turned up as I could also hear motorbikes starting as some of them left. Well, what did you want me to do, arrest them all for drink driving or chase them on my pedal bike? Anyway, drink driving was ok in those days so long as you did not go over the top and ram the Chief Constable's car or kill someone other than yourself. As I guided another few stragglers out of the front door I felt Imelda's hand hook into my arm. 'Can you walk me home officer, it's dark out there and after all, it is your duty to protect the public?'

She smiled with that mischievous look she had perfected. Always a slight hint of sarcasm in everything she said but not in a cruel way.

'Well if we can leave your friends to finish up here then, of course, Miss Poole. You shall have police protection for the walk home.'

Imelda lived with her mother and sisters at Little Steeping farm on the very edge of the village. It would only take me ten minutes and I was now desperate to get back to my bed. The pleasure of a walk with Imelda sounded like the perfect end to a shit day. As we turned to leave she shouted to the boys,

'Guys, this kind policeman is going to walk me up the road, I will come back around in the morning to check if Steven is ok and try to clean up. God help him when his parents get back on Monday and see the state of this place. If you two are not still drunk, you could consider helping me tomorrow?'

The last few words were said in a tone that made it obvious that Imelda knew she would be cleaning up the house by herself in the morning. I had expected Carl to comment on me stealing his girlfriend, but he just gave me a drunken smile. He was too good looking and confident in himself to have any doubts that every woman would fall at his feet. No, it was Robbie who gave me a look that said it all. I wondered if he usually escorted Imelda back from parties while Carl stayed behind to admire himself in the mirror.

We walked down the dimly lit village road towards Little Steeping farm. Imelda clutched her arm around mine as we strolled along. In broad daylight that would have been a problem, but it was now after two in the morning and trust me, even that old fruitcake Ma Capley would be asleep by now. She would probably be dreaming up new ways to annoy me. As we reached the edge of the village street lights and near darkness, Imelda suddenly stopped and turned to me. 'Gordon, can I tell you something?' For once she sounded deadly serious and it made me pay attention and look her in the eyes.

'Yes, Miss Poole, what is it? Are you going to confess that it was you who phoned up and called me a cock? It's ok I forgive you but if you do it again I shall have to report it to the police.'

She laughed before replying.

'Well, you would have to report it to the police Gordon because the whole village knows you are not a proper policeman.'

'What the fuck do you mean by that Miss Poole?' She was still chuckling good-naturedly as she continued to take the mickey.

'Come on Gordon, my mum says you spend most

of your time in The Oak. I bet this is the first call out you have had to do since you started in the village. I reckon that's why most of the folks like you. It's because you do absolutely fuck all.'

I had to laugh at this confident blue-eyed young woman putting me in my place but in a nice way.

'Anyway, it was Steven who phoned up and called you a cock. Carl and Robbie thought it was funny, but I didn't.'

'Why was that then Miss Poole?'

'It's because I like you, Gordon, I really do. You don't seem like a cock at all even if Steven thinks you are. And if you keep calling me Miss Poole I will walk the rest of the way without you'

Like a big idiot, my face went red. Here I was, a 22-year-old burly big policeman feeling intimidated by a young girl who was half my height. But that was Imelda, she always made me feel that way. Suddenly she stopped laughing.

'Gordon I am serious, there is something you need to know.'

I could see she meant it, so I cut the wisecracks out and tried to be serious. What happened next is another of those odd little incidents in life that stick with you forever and make you smile when you think of them years later. Before Imelda started to speak again she reached into her little handbag and pulled out a half-smoked joint. Without even the merest hint of self-consciousness or doubt, she lit it and inhaled deeply before handing it to me. She then burst out laughing at the look of shock on my face.

'For Christ sake Gordon, it's a fucking joint, not a syringe, take a pull, you might need it when I tell you this.

'It's not that Imelda, well Christ you are only sixteen and I am a policeman. Jesus, I am even in uniform. If anyone sees me smoking a joint in the street with a juvenile I will be out of a job.'

'Bloody hell Gordon, you make such a fuss about nothing. Anyway, it's pitch black, who the hell is going to see you? Do you want a smoke of this or not?' I inhaled the joint, well come on, did you really think I was an angel. It was 1978, I was only 22 and anyway, all the older nightshift cops at that time were probably sitting in the back of some pub in Ludlow getting pissed. I could feel the fuzziness of the joint taking effect while Imelda acted as though getting stoned in the street with a policeman was a perfectly normal part of her day.

'Do you remember a few years back, the supposed break-in up at Deadwater house? Imelda had gone back to looking serious, a worried frown for once crossing that face with the blue eyes and endless curls. Now she suddenly had my interest, even the effects of the joint suddenly wore off.

'Go on' I said, trying not to sound too desperate to hear what would come next.'

'It was us, me and Carl, Robbie and Steven. We went up that day because Robbie seemed convinced that the Denham-Grangers were keeping their secret child locked in the back room.'

'It's ok Imelda, there is no need to worry, it is forgotten about now, maybe best to keep it under your hat. Thanks for telli…,' she cut me off abruptly.

'No, it's not that, I don't give a fuck about what the Denham-Grangers think or what PC Gordon thinks, it's the other stuff that followed.'

'What other stuff, tell me, Imelda?' By now, I was really starting to listen.

'Well from that day, Robbie has been convinced that something was in the room and he saw it. It is not as though he has ever wavered from the story, he is sure that someone was imprisoned in that house and they spoke to him.'

I felt slightly disappointed by this revelation as it was hardly new to me. Old Davington had often repeated the story in The Oak although as you would expect, he did not mention the names of those involved. 'Well Imelda, if Robbie is convinced then there is little you or I can do about it. One thing is for sure I am not going anywhere near the Denham-Grangers with that accusation, they would eat me alive.

'That is not the only thing Gordon, there is something else.' I listened as Imelda took another draw on the joint and looked into my eyes. 'Recently Steven has been telling the rest of us that something is watching him, something from the house. I don't know what it is, but it is not a person, well it's not alive that's for sure. Robbie reckons it is because we let it out of Deadwater house when he pushed the window open.'

I looked back at her wondering if Imelda really was as smart as I thought she was. Steven was off his marbles, of that I was sure and Robbie, well maybe he had got a fright that day and the illusion had become real in his head. 'Christ Imelda are you kidding me, maybe you should leave off smoking the drugs.' For the first time, I saw anger flash across her face, a look that made it obvious that I was the fool and not her. Her words were sharp and cutting

'For God's sake Gordon, listen to what I am trying to tell you. I have seen it as well, why the hell do you think I wanted you to walk me home.'

'Ok, ok Imelda. I am sorry, it's just a bit hard to take in all this stuff about ghosts and dead children. The Denham-Grangers seem fairly normal to me.'

Imelda stared back and then her anger dissipated, and she smiled. She stretched up on her toes and kissed me on the lips. 'Thanks for walking me home

Constable Chisholm. Oh, and thanks also for letting Steven go.'

And then she turned and quickly disappeared into the night up the track to Little Steeping farm. So, you see after the party, that was the second thing I remember from 1978. Not the story of the ghost of Deadwater, that would start to seep into my very being year after year. No, it was walking Imelda back home that night and her kissing me. It would be a few years before I would even talk to her again, but like the ghost, she too had touched the very core of my soul.

Thoughts:

We left a quaint English country village when I was seven to move to Belfast just as the troubles were brewing. To say that I did not fit in would be an understatement. My accent in an inner-city Irish Catholic school was never going to be a winner. I would like to pretend that it made me into a man, but I would be lying. Instead, I stayed under the radar and other than a few beatings from the bullies and teachers I got by. Funny how even at that age I understood to keep away from the priest though, maybe I really was smarter than they gave me credit for.

4

SAY GOODBYE

(Deadwater House 1957)

Old man Denham Granger lay propped up in his bed. The large austere bedroom with its oak furniture reflected his status as the owner of Deadwater, the master of the house. This was the first time in days that he had been left alone, no doctors fussing around and his eldest son John away to Ludlow with Roberta for the day. The only one he enjoyed seeing in his room was Martin Dornan the general manager of his still thriving business. Leonard knew he was approaching the end, but he could still not let go completely. It made him feel good when Martin came to see him. His long-serving associate was making the decisions now although his son John would still have to sign everything off. Despite being bedridden for the last year, the old man would still try to keep an overall view of how things were going.

He bitterly resented Harry for walking out after the fight seven years previously, more so with every passing month and no word from him. And now it was too late, the old man accepted that the elder boy would have to take over. And yet there had been a surprisingly fortuitous turn of events in the last two years and it was called Roberta De Crecco. Leonard knew that she was the reason why John had started to at least take some responsibility, she was driving his decisions and at last making something of a man of him. The old man understood that life was really a business and if you tried to run everything with business rules then things would work out. That is why he respected Roberta although he did not like her. Leonard understood exactly what she was. A middle-class girl with little money and massive aspirations. He knew she had simply taken over John's life and married him to get Deadwater, to get the business. She was just like the old man, do what you must do to win. So, they respected each other as equals but that was as far as any real affection would ever go.

As he considered things the old man smiled to himself, a rare thing but he could not help it. *Well if it takes a money grabbing call girl to make a man of that lady's boy of mine then so be it. If it must be her that keeps Denham Granger Metals going what does it matter, so long as the business continues.* He turned to push the pillows away as the pain swept through his body again and tried to get some sleep. The pills started to take effect as Leonard drifted into his dreams. The same vision as always, Roberta and John smiling in front of him while in the distance Harry watched and waited. The old man was suddenly awake, he felt different. In fact, he was not sure if anything was real or maybe he was still dreaming. The room floated around his head, everything felt grey and mixed up.

John and Roberta sat facing each other in the main sitting room. Neither said a word, they did not need to. They both knew the end had arrived for the old man. Since they had returned from Ludlow a few days ago he had taken another bad turn and had been drifting in and out of consciousness. The two of them jumped as the doctor pushed open the door that led to the stairs. 'John, I think it might be best if you go up to see your father now.'

'Is he, is he...?'

'Yes, it is only a matter of hours, if that,' replied the doctor.

Despite not being invited to join her husband to go upstairs Roberta ignored the doctor's instructions and walked with authority by John's side. The room had that stillness that seems to pervade the air when death is near. It is almost as if all human sound falls away and the only thing left is the faint resonance of a person's last breaths. Ironically the only time in life when we totally forget ourselves and focus entirely on another human being. John politely asked their trusty housekeeper to leave him and Roberta alone with the old man. The elder son took his father's hand and held it in his. Roberta was surprised to see tears falling down John's face, she had never felt that old Leonard was close to anyone other than his business. But that was John, always fragile, always the first to break down when anything untoward happened. And yet in her way, Roberta loved her husband, not with any passion but as a solid business proposition at least. She respected him more for what he had than what he was.

John let go of his father's hand and stood up to start pacing the room back and forth, 'Sorry Roberta dear, I can't stand to see the old man like this, it is simply just too much. I rather liked him better when he was bawling me out.' Roberta recognised the sign that John was ready to run as he always did in any crisis. She had watched him do the same with every difficult situation he had ever encountered in his life. He would stand up and walk the floor while wringing his hands together. This would usually end up with him going for a smoke until the issue resolved itself or someone else made a decision.

'Why don't you go and have a smoke, my dear? I know this must be simply awful for you. I will stay here and watch your father if you want to tell Doctor Langton to come back up?'

'Oh, if you think that's best then Roberta. You really are a love. I, I will have a quick smoke, calm the old nerves and then come back up.'

John quietly closed the door leaving Roberta sat on her chair next to the old man's bed. She listened for Johns footsteps going down the flight of stairs and then leaned forward until her face was inches away from old Denham-Granger. She was just close enough to hear his last dying breath as she whispered,

'Before you go, Leonard, I must tell you something. Tomorrow I will instruct John to set in motion my plans to sell the company. We would both prefer to enjoy the money rather than have to work. You know as well as I do Leonard that your son will mess things up in the long run. It really makes far more sense to close the whole operation down and get what we can.' She took the old man's dead hand into hers before continuing.

'I hope you don't take this badly Leonard, after all, you more than anyone must know that this is just simply a business decision.'

And then she smiled and patted the old man's head before reaching over to close his vacant staring eyes.

***

(Witton Saint James 1980)

Months could pass in my role as the Witton Saint James police constable with very little to do. It became a routine for me to either wander through the village during the day talking to the locals and getting the gossip or working a late shift and doing a bit of night time patrolling. The latter would sometimes find me listening at the supposedly locked up door of The Oak around eleven o'clock. I would check to see if they had closed at ten as was required by the law. If I heard voices from inside I would rattle the outer doors with my truncheon. The noise inside would stop as the drinkers waited in anticipation to see who it was. Big Bill Tavey, the Landlord would start the process of unbolting the outer and inner door. Then with a sheepish look, he would peer into the darkness, 'Ahh if it's, not young Constable Gordon Chisholme.' I would walk in, give a nod to the huddled drinkers and take my police helmet off'

'Just your usual young Gordon, a pint of Worthington?'

'Yes, please Bill, I have been looking forward to this all day. Can you give me change of a pound for the cigarette machine as well mate?'

And that really is as exciting as it got most of the time. Even if a little crime was being committed such as breaking the licensing laws I was fucked if I was going to do anything about it. Well, it was still only 1980 and anyway Big Bill gave me free beer, that was the agreement.

But that year did not pass without tragedy, I suppose that is why I remember it so well. Two things stick in my memory, the first was my second visit up to Deadwater House. I had not been to see the Denham-Grangers since my easy-going chat with John five years previously in 1975. Somehow, I had never got around to reporting back on the supposed window incident after Roberta had breezed into my little police station. If I am honest I had been putting off going back to see the Denham-Grangers because like the rest of the village I was in awe of the people in the big house. This time I had no choice but to go and see them after I got a call one morning from Malachy Proctor the gravedigger at Saint John's on the Mound church. He had phoned me to report vandalism to one of the headstones in the graveyard. I pulled into the car park and could see Malachy leaning on his spade as he took a rest from digging holes for the dead.

'Good morning Mr. Proctor. My name is PC Chisholme, you reported some damage to a grave?'

'I did that, but please call me Malachy young sir.' He edged up right beside me, one of those people who have no understanding of respecting others personal space.

'Ok Malachy, well I am Gordon, it's nice to meet you. So which gravestone is damaged then?'

He walked me over to a headstone that had deep score marks across the front. He was so close to me that I was almost expecting him to try and hold my hand.

'It is Old Leonard Denham-Granger's grave young Gordon. No idea why anyone would want to damage it.' The letters on the headstone had almost been chiselled out, it was as if someone had a grudge against the name of the old man. I knelt to take a closer look before replying.

'Ok Malachy, well it is unlikely that we will find out who did it, but I suppose I had better go up to Deadwater and report it to the Denham-Grangers anyway.' The gravedigger edged back closer to me again.

'Tis a shame anyone would do this cos old Leonard was well respected. He had a difficult time with his boys. Harry was the scourge of every girl in the village when he was young. Rumour is he got more than a few pregnant. Never liked Harry to be honest, too volatile. Liked the older boy John, I heard he preferred the company of men. How about you young Gordon, do you prefer the company of men?'

By now I was starting to feel a bit uncomfortable in the company of old Malachy never mind any other men. I was getting a distinct impression that he was trying to chat me up. Don't get me wrong, I am not homophobic, I would have been ill at ease even if a female stranger had tried the same thing. Well, maybe not if it had been Britt Ekland or Sophia Loren but you get my point.

'Erm, right Mister Proctor, I mean Malachy, I need to rush. Thanks for reporting this.'

'No need to rush young Gordon, come on into the church and I will make you a nice cup of tea.'

'No, it is ok Malachy, I am on duty and have other calls to make,' I lied. Without thinking I held out my hand to shake his and make my getaway. He grasped it and held on for what was probably only a few seconds, but it seemed like an eternity.

'Well that is a pity young Gordon, I have some lovely scones that Bobby made for my lunch. I could have shared them with you. Within seconds I was back on my peddle bike while making a mental note never to respond to a call from the Witton Saint James grave digger again.

I decided to cycle up to Deadwater straight away and let them know about the damaged gravestone. As I arrived the first thing I noticed was that the garden looked uncared for, so different from my previous visit half a decade ago. Some maintenance must have been done but only enough to keep it from getting out of control. It seemed that the rumours in the village about the Denham-Grangers running out of money might be true.

I rang the bell and stepped back, police helmet held with reverence in my hand. I was surprised when Roberta answered the door, *so they really did no longer have any servants*. She looked much older than when I had last seen her. The well dressed and confident woman who had stormed into the police station four years previously now looked dishevelled and careworn. I suppose I just put it down to her being 54 and assumed time had caught up with the lady of Deadwater. She showed me politely into the sitting room and went to look for John. Even for 1980, the room looked as though it was trapped in a time warp. The fittings and furniture would be the same as when the old man ruled the house. It still looked grand but somehow it also looked tired.

One of the several doors into the room opened and in walked John Denham-Granger. He looked the same, unlike his wife he had hardly aged in the four years but something about his demeanour had changed. He did look rougher though, he had the face of a hardened drinker. Although he carried or tried to carry the same friendly tone, his eyes looked different, they no longer held that soft easy-going sparkle they seemed to have last time I had visited. 'Ahh Gordon, it is nice to see you, young man, how can I help? Have the lovely inhabitants of Witton Saint James sent you to check up on us then?' The bitterness in his tone seemed so much at odds with the John

Denham-Granger I had met before.

'No, No John, it is an official visit, unfortunately. I was at the church this morning and it seems your father's headstone has been damaged. Probably just children messing around, but I thought it best that I let you know'. His reaction took me by surprise as he suddenly dropped any pretence of being friendly.

'So, the vermin in the village are not just content with trespassing at my home, now they are desecrating our graves as well?' He looked at me, almost as if he wanted a challenge, as though he was angry with something and it was my fault.

'Well John, I am sure that is not true. It is probably just a coincidence, kids playing around. No doubt it could have been any gravestone and you have just been unlucky.'

'My name is fucking Mr. Denham-Granger to you. Now if you are finished could you please leave. Maybe you could pass on the message to the rest of the village that they are not welcome anywhere near Deadwater House.' I was totally taken aback by his anger, this had been so unlike my previous visit. At that point, Roberta walked into the room, almost too quickly as though she was anxious but not wanting to show it. Like John, she seemed tense and I could see the lines that crossed her face, worry lines that matched the demeanour of both her and her husband.

'Let me show you out Constable, what was the

name again?'

'Gordon Chisholme, Mrs. Denham-Granger, you can call me Gordon though, everyone in the village does.' I tried to smile despite the tense atmosphere that seemed to pervade Deadwater house.

'Let me see you to the door Constable if you are finished with your visit?'

It was almost as if Roberta was desperate to get me away from John as quickly as possible. He seemed so different, what had happened to the friendly easy going almost effeminate John I had met only five years previously. What had made him so angry, angry with the world, with me, with the village?'

'I am sorry constable, what was the name again? Oh yes, Gordon. I am sorry Gordon if John came across a bit sharp with you. He has not been too well over the last few years, rather feels the world has conspired against him. Please accept my apologies if we seem unfriendly. To be honest we would prefer if you and the rest of the villagers would just leave us to ourselves if that is ok? And with that, she closed the door leaving me feeling bewildered and a little insulted. As I walked down the steps I picked up my bike and out of respect wheeled it down the gravel road that led away from Deadwater House. My head told me not to turn and look back, *don't perpetuate the myth Gordon, keep walking away*. But I knew I had to look and see, the same as I had done five years previously. Somehow, I knew the watcher would be there in the window, but this time it did not hide, this time it did not feel like the person it had been. Now it was something else, something evil but still something I would not accept as real. Just a figment of my imagination, the same as the rest of the village gossips.

As I cycled down to the road I remember thinking *thank God they have given me an excuse to never have to come back to this place again.* Of course, that is not how things would work out. At the time I did not realise that the visit was just the start of years of animosity I would endure from the very much changed John Denham-Granger.

The Deadwater house trip was difficult but nothing compared to my other memory of that year. It was a Sunday evening and I was just settling down to watch Dallas on the TV. I was in a good mood having enjoyed a day off without some old bag in the village phoning up to complain about a dead fox in the road or teenagers drinking inside the bus shelter. JR Ewing had just done the dirty on his brother again and I was contemplating a free beer at The Oak when the bloody phone rang. It could only be two things, my mother checking I had fed myself or some old nut cake like Ma Capley who hated me having an evening off. It was neither, the voice on the end of the phone was Ray Warton the father of that little runt Steven. 'Gordon, would you be able to come up to number

12, something is not right. I and Annie have just got back from Birmingham, something is wrong. Steven's motorbike is here, and I can hear his music, but he will not answer the door. I can't get the key in the front or back as he has put the bolts on. Would you come, Gordon, would you come, please, to number 12'?

I could sense the anxiety in Ray's voice as he was throwing the words out without taking a breath. It was as though he wanted me to instantly solve the problem, whatever it was.

'Give me ten minutes Mr. Warton and I will be straight over.'

'Thanks, Gordon, thanks, we will wait at the garden gate for you, number 12, it's number 12.'

I felt like laughing as I put on my uniform when I thought about Ray repeating his address to me. I knew number 12 better than most houses in the village. Every time Stevens parent's left to go away for the weekend I would be up at the house for some reason. Either a party that got out of hand or underaged drinking and maybe some sort of drugs. Since his friends Carl and Imelda had gone off to college Steven had become the drink and drug baron for all the other loose kids in the village. Even Robbie had a job at the Stokely's garage and was working with him and his sons as an apprentice mechanic. Don't get me wrong, Steven was hardly a big-time criminal, just a teenager who had lost his way, but as each month passed he seemed to get more troublesome and withdrawn.

I arrived at number 12 as darkness fell to find Ray and his wife Annie sitting in the family Austin Allegro, the perfect middle-class village couple, everything in order except for the delinquent son. Ray stepped out of the car to greet me, he looked worried, concerned. Annie stayed in the car, I sensed they knew more about the gravity of the situation than me. I was thinking, *I bet JR screws Bobby Ewing over again and I am missing it because that little toe rag Steven can't handle a strong joint.*

'Gordon, I know you probably think we are overreacting but even if Steven is asleep or wasted, I have banged the hell out of the door and no answer.'

'It's ok Ray try not to worry, I am sure he probably has the music turned up so loud he would not hear Concorde if it landed on the roof.' The flippant reply made Ray gently take me by the shoulders.

'Gordon you need to know, we have had problems over the years with Steven. He can go into really dark moods; the slightest thing can get him down. One minute he is fine and the next he won't speak to anyone. Anyway, we are not stupid, we know you have been here when we are away because of trouble. Old Ma Capley is forever knocking our door to complain about what goes on when Steven is left on his own.'

The words took me by surprise and suddenly I was no longer thinking about JR and Bobby on the tv, in fact, even Sue Ellen had left my thoughts as it suddenly dawned on me that I could be in the middle of a real crisis. I told Ray to get back in the car with Annie and explained I might have to break in if Steven did not come to the door. He accepted my invitation almost with resignation as though he had grown weary of the problems his son was causing them. I walked around to the back of the house and pressed my ear against the locked door. All the lights in the house were out. Ashes to Ashes by David Bowie was playing on repeat on Steven's record player. I decided to boot the door down to the accompaniment of David singing, *Ashes to Ashes, Funk to Funky, we know Major Tom's a junkie*. The frame gave way with surprising ease, it made me feel like a real policeman for a change.

I edged through the broken door into the pitch-black kitchen while cursing myself for not bringing a torch. Why is it always so bloody difficult to find a light switch in the dark? My hand wandered all over the wall until it reached an opening and then shot forward with momentum as it hit an empty space. Before I could pull back I realised I had touched something, something wet. I shrieked as whatever it was brushed past me towards the open door. 'For fuck sake, is that you Steven, stop pissing around you little shit.' In a total panic, I finally found the light switch and the kitchen suddenly lit up. The room was empty, nothing, not even a sound. *Pull yourself together Gordon for Christ sake.* I will admit though, I was spooked. On the kitchen floor, small drops of slime trailed out into the garden.

I grabbed a glass of water from the sink before resuming my search. I checked the rest of the downstairs rooms just in case although instinct told me that whatever I was going to see would be on the floor above in Steven's room. I reached the bottom of the stairs and somehow knew I would not have to go any further to find what I had come for. My head slowly looked up the staircase to the landing at the top of the house and there he was. Swinging grotesquely from a rope attached to the open attic panel was the chalk white body of the already dead Warton boy.

I don't know about you, but it always feels wrong to me when funerals are held on a bright sunny day. It makes those present want to chat and you sometimes forget you are supposed to act depressed and sad. I stood in the glaring sun at the little gate leading up to Saint John's on the Mound church. I was dressed in my police uniform almost like a guard of honour for those arriving. Of course, the whole village had turned out. They might not have been too keen on Steven as a person, but everyone recognised how sad it was that someone as young as 18 had taken their own life. His friends Imelda, Carl and Robbie were there but things had changed even for them. Carl had his latest girlfriend with him, a stunning blonde who held tightly onto his arm. I wondered to myself if she held the mirror for him while he combed his own long black hair. Robbie as always was without a partner and walked past with his parents. It was Imelda who seemed to have changed the most. She walked beside her then-boyfriend, probably someone from college. Her younger sisters and mother following in her footsteps. In the two years since I had seen her, she had grown into a beautiful woman and looked even more amazing than I remembered. Her black dress and hat adding to the sophistication and charm as the long dark curls tumbled down her back.

As they passed I nodded a polite hello to the group. I think I was as taken aback as the rest of the family when Imelda told them she wanted to ask the policeman something and to walk on until she caught up. Imelda came up close to me and smiled.

'Hi Gordon, it has been a long time. I did mean to explain things after you walked me home a few years back but…well you know life took over.'

'Oh yes, no don't worry Imelda, I had forgotten all about that night,' I lied. She smiled at me but this time with a glint in her eyes that said, I know you are lying. 'So, you still doing illegal drugs then Imelda?' I was sorry I had said the words the minute they came out, she just seemed to make me nervous. I was in love I suppose but would not admit it.

'Why, are you trying to sell me some constable?' Her joke broke the ice and put us on level terms.

'Imelda, I am really sorry about Steven, I know you were good friends and tended to look after him when he got into trouble.'

'Thanks, Gordon, but you don't need to overdo it. I know you did not like him, and he could be a little shit at times, but you stick by your friends. Sometimes that is just the way it has to be.'

'We had better get in Imelda, I think that is most of the folks here and the service will start soon.'

She looked directly into my eyes, 'Yes, ok, but I need a chat with you Gordon, in private. I am only home for a few days before I go back to college. Can I come over and see you, maybe tomorrow evening? We need to talk, finish what we started two years ago.' I flushed, it was a perfectly innocent comment, but Imelda always made me feel like an idiot, I never knew how to react.

'Don't worry Mister Policeman, it's official business, I won't jump on your bones or force you to smoke a joint. Not unless you want me to that is. Anyway, my boyfriend, Trev is home with me and he might get jealous'

'Yes, yes of course Imelda. What time suits you?'

She had her serious face on now.

'That's perfect, I will be there at seven. Look, Gordon, I am not joking with you. You need to know what's going on.' I nodded a yes back to her rather than put my foot in it again. She poked me in the ribs and laughed.

'It really is good to see you again PC Chisholme.'

And with that cheeky Imelda smile, she walked off towards the church.

The service passed as all these services do with the immediate family isolated in devastation while those on the periphery check their watches and think, *that's 40 minutes now, almost done, these things never go on for more than an hour.* And then comes the awful bit, the family stand at the back of the church, tears falling while the rest of the mourners shake their hand and repeat the same words over and over. *Really sad about your loss, such a nice ceremony, he will be dearly missed.*

Oh, I nearly forgot to mention, too busy reminiscing about Imelda that day. Halfway through the funeral service the door at the back of the church abruptly rattled open. In walked a dishevelled looking John Denham-Granger, he seemed drunk as he staggered to lean against the wall at the back. I was thinking, well maybe that is a nice gesture, *the guy from the big house at least coming to pay his respect.* But the real impression he gave was that he was there to gloat, to look down on the villagers in their hour of torment, as though to say,

Well, why should I be the only one to suffer, let me see how you enjoy being the victim for a change.

Not that I really noticed too much. I kept thinking about Imelda who stood a few rows in front of me with her dopey boyfriend Trev. Once or twice she turned around and smiled at me. I decided that even a funeral or an angry Denham-Granger was not going to spoil my day.

Thoughts:

When I was young I both feared and respected the police. The fact was in those days Policemen were mostly male as well as tall imposing characters not to be messed with. They also investigated most crimes including housebreaking. Please don't take this as me being sexist but when you call the Police these days it's usually a couple of five-foot females who turn up. They don't follow up on housebreaking anymore, but you can bet they will descend on you in a flash if someone reports you being sexist. They would come to arrest me, and I would be thinking, *so a couple of tiny females what are you going to do to me then girls?* The next minute I would be shaking around the floor like a jelly after being Tasered. I suppose that is why they don't need big daft male policemen anymore.

5

I WATCH YOU SLEEP

(Deadwater House 1975)

The death of old man Leonard Denham-Granger really heralded the end of ambition for his elder son John. It probably also ended any pretence that John and Roberta had married for any other reason than it was convenient and suited both their needs. Once the business was sold and the couple had the money to play with they could live out their fantasy of being the Lord and Lady of the big house without really having to do anything. John followed up on his dream of being a poet but that only lasted a few years and truth be told, he really wasn't very good at it. He could afford to be published but the reality was he sold hardly anything, so it proved to be just an expensive hobby. Once any pretence of having a profession had gone John was able to pursue his real passion in life.

Doing very little other than drink and indulge in the occasional mild drug use when he could get hold of them in London. Oh and of course pay for male company once he was in the city and out of sight of his wife.

Roberta also embraced the life of the entitled lady. She would spend half of her time at Deadwater fussing over the house and John and the other half in London enjoying her mostly female friends. As the fifties evolved into the exciting sixties Roberta continued being a socialite with little regard to how much she was spending. She knew her husband preferred men and the fact was it did not bother her in the least. They had never really consummated the marriage and Roberta had simply got used to a life of celibacy. It was something she preferred not to think about although she still received plenty of attention from male admirers and enjoyed flirting. But that was as far as it would go, she was far too smart to risk the perfect life she had. She respected John as a friend as well as the provider of Deadwater House and the Denham-Granger money.

The first cracks in their idyllic lifestyle started as the swinging sixties came to an end and by the early seventies, Roberta knew they could not continue to throw money around the way they had previously. Both her and John's visits to London started to dry up and as they reached their fifties they spent more time at Deadwater. The once large staff was now reduced to just two full-time heads. Old Maud the housekeeper from Leonards days remained. She was well into her seventies and could no longer do many of her previous chores. Roberta kept her on more for the company than anything else. The garden was looked after by Toby Bowman who lived on one of the nearby farms. He tried his best to cover the work that had previously been done by as many as four gardeners, but he was slowly losing the battle against nature. While he was able to keep the lawns and flower beds close to the house under control, much of the peripheral garden area had disappeared under overgrown bushes and trees. Roberta would potter about the garden, but it was mostly to cut flowers for the house or to give Toby more work to do. The large and previously well-maintained building started to look its age as money was no longer spent on repairs. As each year passed the Denham-Grangers would close more of the rooms up and let the dust and spiders have the space to themselves. But the couple where still happy enough, age dulls ambition and we all settle into a routine. John with his half bottle of port each day and the occasional joint when Toby the gardener could supply it. Roberta with her now very sporadic visits to London. They rarely went into the village unless it was necessary. Old Maud would be sent in for the groceries and Roberta might occasionally visit the post office but other than that they kept their distance.

And that is how things might have carried on, the Denham-Grangers slowly slipping into old age and senility while the villagers quietly forgot about them, but it was not to be. One blustery Autumn day in 1975 as the leaves swirled in the wind and fell onto the grass beneath Deadwater a taxi pulled into the drive. From that moment on everything changed, for the house, for the village and even for me. How was I to know that as I unlocked the police station door for the first time that events up at the big house had already cast a shadow over my life in Witton Saint James?

Roberta was giving more orders to the already overworked gardener when she saw the taxi coming up the driveway that looped in front of the house. They rarely had visitors. Her sister was the last one a few years before but now they tended to meet in London to make the journey to see her ageing mother. *It has got to have taken a wrong turning, who would come to see us in a taxi of all things?* But even as she tried to convince herself Roberta had a sinking feeling that change had arrived and maybe not for the better. A tall figure stepped out of the car holding a suitcase and with sudden disbelief Roberta thought it was John, but that was impossible, he was in the house. As the man walked towards her he smiled, she knew straight away that it was him. The brother John had told her about, somehow, they had always known that one day he would come looking for his share and here he was.'

Good afternoon. I take it you are the famous Roberta Denham-Granger no less? May I introduce myself, I am Harry, Harry Denham-Granger, the brother of your husband John. I am sorry for turning up like this, but it is my family home after all. Is John in my dear?'

Roberta surveyed the apparition in front of her. He looked so like John but somehow more rugged. His cropped hair was unusual for the mid-seventies and his face supported a full beard. It was as if John was standing there and had made a poor attempt to disguise himself. But that was where the similarity ended. This man had a steely resolve and a confidence bordering on arrogance. It was obvious that he could handle himself, his eyes looked through you as though he was looking for a challenge. A flicker of danger, a hint of pent-up anger. And for the first time in her life, Roberta felt her emotions unwind, for the first time she gave ground to a man and let him start to take control.

John and Harry sat facing each other in front of the large fire in the ornate sitting room. The elder brother had opened one of his prized vintage malt whisky bottles to toast his brothers return, or was it to dull the pain?

'But why are you running from these people old boy? What could you have done that is so awful they would want to see you dead?' John asked the question with incredulity, this was straight out of a novel surely. His sheltered life could not perceive anything beyond afternoon tea and a half bottle of port following a stroll in the garden.

'For fuck sake John, there is a big world out there. How the hell do you think I survived without the family money for the last 25 years. I told you, I got involved with people who would kill their own mother if the money was good. What in fucks name did you expect me to do on the other side of the world, drive a fucking bus? John fidgeted in his seat as he realised that the years had not made Harry any less angry with the world.

Ok, Ok Harry, but Jesus it's rather a lot to take in at one go old boy, a bit of a rum do if you don't mind me saying. How can you be sure they won't track you here? If this cartel as you call it is so widespread then they might find you here. Roberta would go positively ape old boy, she really would.

Harry wanted to laugh, listening to his older brother was like going back to 1950, he had not changed one bit, no development or maturity. The sheltered life of Deadwater House seemed to have preserved his elder sibling the way those glass jars keep dead organs pickled for an eternity.

'Trust me, John, this was the one thing I always kept hidden. The insurance policy I knew I would need one day. You don't retire from the cartel; your time simply runs out. To them I am Tony Brendon, no one knows anything about my upbringing as a Denham-Granger.' Harry leaned forward and looked into John's eyes.

'Let me make this plain to you John. I fucked them over, they sent a hitman to get rid of me. My usefulness was at an end. I got lucky, the fuckers gun jammed, and I damn near took his head off with a machete. They know I flew back to London from Hong Kong and they know I have enough detail and names to cause real shit for them. They will do everything to track me down and kill me, and that means you and Roberta as well. Give me a year hidden here and it will die down. Anyway, you owe me John, half that old bastard's money should be mine.'

John shuffled in his seat, he looked tormented. Harry had always been trouble, and nothing had changed. All this talk of gangs and murder was too much for him to take in.

'Ok old boy. Well look I trust Maud the housekeeper with my life, so she won't say a word. The only other regular is the gardener but he never comes into the house. God, I don't know how Roberta will handle this, it's a bit much old boy, jeez it really is. Are you absolutely sure they won't track you here? I mean this could put all three of us in a right old pickle.' A flash of anger and impatience crossed Harry's face.

'John, for fuck sake, will you fucking listen to what I am saying. Even if I leave here and get caught they will torture me to find out where I have been. Once they get to know about my background you and everyone in Deadwater will need to die. You have no fucking choice, John. Let me hide here and pray they don't locate me, or we are all dead.' As if to emphasise his point Harry reached into the coat he had hung over the back of the chair. He pulled out a small pistol and pointed it at his older brother.

'Do you think I carry this around for a laugh John? I have killed men with it before. Do I have to fucking shoot you before you will believe what I am telling you?' John looked at his erratic brother with fear in his eyes.

'Jesus Christ Harry, ok, ok, I believe you. Please stop pointing that thing at me, you are making me a tad nervous old chap. I rather think guns are best kept for the grouse shoot don't you think?' Harry burst out laughing while shaking his head as though he was talking to a child. He passed the gun from hand to hand as if to emphasise that he was the man in control of Deadwater now, whether Master John liked it or not. Finally, he replaced the gun into his coat before talking again.

'John, you really are something else. How the fuck did you ever manage to get yourself a woman? Not only that, you got a looker as well. What was up, did all your male friends get fed up with you?'

The older brother was rescued from the uncomfortable situation when Roberta walked back into the room. John had his back to her at the fire while Harry watched as she came towards the two brothers. Their eyes met and lingered for longer than would be normal for two virtual strangers. John swivelled round to face his wife, already he was starting to feel that Harry was going to come between them. Roberta broke the tension by returning the conversation to more mundane matters.

'Maud has set up a room in the West Wing for you Harry. We will need to get an electrician in to do some re-wiring as the upstairs rooms have been closed off for a while. The bed has been made up and we found an oil heater to warm it up until we can get things sorted out.'

'That is very good of you Roberta, how on earth did John ever discover a woman as smart as you? Harry stood up to face Mrs. Denham-Granger.

'Roberta, I am trying to convince this dumb husband of yours that he needs to keep it a secret that I am here. Can I trust you to do the same Roberta, and what about the housekeeper Maud?'

'Of course, you can Harry. I fully understand and trust me, Maud will do exactly as I say.' She reached out and touched Harry's arm before continuing.

'We will make your stay as comfortable as we can Harry and for as long as you need.' Harry caught Roberta's eyes as he replied.

'Oh, I know you will Roberta. It is that brother of mine that I am worried about.' He patted John condescendingly on the head. John stood up as if he was trying to show them both that he was still the master of the house.

'Roberta darling, could we retire to the dining room and have a little chat, my dear? Harry help yourself to another whisky old chap, shan't be too long.'

Harry watched the retreating figure of Roberta and his brother walk off towards the door. *Not bad for a woman approaching fifty, not bad at all,* he thought to himself. Harry bent down to pour another whisky into his empty glass and chuckled. *A few years holed up in this fucking place again might be fun. Stick it out Harry and when the trail has gone cold I can get my share of the inheritance and start again. Maybe even have a bit of fun with Johns old girl while I am here.* He raised his glass as if giving a toast and whispered the words,

'To Harry Denham-Granger, welcome back to Deadwater.'

***

(Witton Saint James 1980)

I ran about the little cottage trying my best to make it presentable at least. Electric fire on, shuffle a cloth around the dust on the window ledges and cabinets, open the windows, fluff the few cushions up. The fact was no matter how much I flounced about she was still going to think it was a dump. It was the day after the funeral and as it approached seven in the evening I expected at any minute Imelda would knock on the door. I knew it was going to be a visit to talk business, but she always made me feel this way. Christ, here I was, a 24-year-old police constable acting like a smitten schoolboy over an 18-year-old.

There was a rattle on the glass. I ran my hand through my hair and straightened up. I took one last look in the mirror, but I still did not look like James Dean. *Calm down Gordon for fuck sake, act cool, try to look sophisticated. Kid yourself that you look like Sean Connery. Shit, what if she needs to use the outside toilet, fuck, it's filthy, too late. Christ, I should have had a drink or a joint to make me more relaxed, this is ridiculous.*

But not as ridiculous as my face must have looked when I opened the door to find Ray Warton the deceased boy's father standing facing me.

'Hi Gordon, I need to speak to you about something, is it ok if I come in? He must have seen the look of utter disappointment on my face as I replied.

'Err yes, Ray, no problem. Could we make it quick though as I have some official business to attend to if that's ok?'

'No problem Gordon, just a quick something I think you should know.'

We sat down on my newly brushed chairs while Ray did most of the talking. It was hard to concentrate knowing that Imelda might be walking to my cottage on the edge of the village at this very moment. I just wanted him to shut up and go but within seconds he had my attention. Funny how the word Deadwater makes my senses become so finely tuned.

'Gordon, my son could be in a dark place sometimes. Steven had these moods that could go up and down within seconds. One minute he would be laughing and joking, the next he would lock himself away in the dark. He could go for days without saying a word. It got worse as he left childhood. Things became hard for me and Annie. But I will tell you something for sure Gordon, something happened that day, he was never the same after that. From then on, he became so depressed and angry with everyone. His poor mother was distraught.'

'What day was that then Mr. Warton?' Of course, I knew exactly the day he was talking about and he sensed it too.'

'Come on Gordon, you know what I am talking about. Four years ago, he and his friends went up to the house, that house. It was just a bunch of fourteen-year-olds having a laugh I suppose, they put a ladder up against the back wall and Denham-Granger chased them. From that day he seemed to go more into his shell, become a problem, always getting into trouble.'

'Mr. Warton, I am sorry, but I don't understand why that would make things worse, what exactly are you trying to tell me?' I could tell he was not giving me the full story. We sat in silence for a few awkward seconds and then he finally got to the point.

'You are going to think I am crazy, Gordon.'

'Let me be the judge of that Ray, tell me what it is and let me decide what to think.' Mr. Warton shuffled about awkwardly in his chair. It was obvious that he felt uncomfortable bringing his dead son's past up. I said nothing further and waited until he had no choice but to continue.

'Well over the last four years Steven had been having terrible nightmares, I mean really traumatic visions. He would wake up screaming sometimes, soaking in sweat. It would take ages to calm him down. I think that's why he spent so much time drinking and smoking drugs, it helped him to keep going and face his worries.' I leaned forward, now giving Ray Warton my full attention. Everything fell silent as I listened intently for him to speak.

'And the nightmares, what were they about?'

'That's the thing Gordon, it was always the same. He would tell me that he would wake up and see a dead person standing beside his bed, looking down at him. He was convinced it was real and not a dream. He seemed to think it was the supposed dead Denham-Granger child grown into a man.'

'And what did you make of all this Ray? Did you think it was just nightmares?

'Yes, Gordon I did, I did. Until one night I heard Steven scream just as I was passing his bedroom door and I burst in. Maybe I was tired and emotional with Stevens health problems, but I swear to God Gordon, I swear for a few seconds I saw it, standing over him, death and decay looking down at my son.'

A loud rattle on the door made me jump about a foot out of my seat. I felt like an idiot as Ray had hardly budged. 'Fuck, sorry Ray. I damn near shit myself there, I was so intent on listening to you.'

Ray stood up to leave as I went to answer the door. 'Imelda, please come in, just let me see Ray off and I will be straight back.' She gave me a look of surprise and came inside.

'Hello Ray, don't let me rush you away, I can wait. It's the least I can do after what you and Annie have been through.'

'No, it's ok Imelda, I did not realise you wanted to

see Gordon as well. I have finished anyway, just heading off. Keep in touch Imelda. I know you and the guys kept an eye to Steven over the years. In fact, you more than anyone looked after him. You were always lovely to my son and we really appreciated it, we really did.' He gave Imelda an affectionate hug and walked out of the door with me close behind him.

I followed the bereaved father down to the end of the cottage path and thanked him for what he had told me. I suppose both of us knew the information meant very little, but I appreciated Ray speaking to me about it anyway. Just as he was about to get into his car he turned around to face me. 'Gordon, I know this probably means nothing but there was one other thing I wanted to mention. It might have nothing to do with this business, but it has been bothering me as well.'

'Yes, Mr. Warton, I mean Ray, what is it?'

'About five years ago, before all this Denham-Granger child rumour nonsense started, yes it would be 1975. I was still working then, doing my electrician stuff. I got called up to Deadwater by that woman Roberta. They wanted mains electricity extended into a couple of rooms they had closed up some years back.'

I was desperate for him to get away, so I could give Imelda my full attention before she started noticing what a dump I lived in. But, I had to hear this next revelation. 'Yes Ray, go on, what happened?'

'Well that's the odd thing, it was weird. It was only the two Denham-Grangers in the house and old Maud Stavely the housekeeper, but I swear to God someone was mucking about with me. I would leave my tools in one place and go downstairs to turn the electricity off and would see the three of them on the ground floor. And yet I would go back upstairs, and my tools would be moved to the other side of the room or put back in the box. A few times I would find my cup empty even though I had just poured it full of tea from my flask. Once I even found my flask had beer in it rather than the tea I know I had filled it with. There was someone else in that house Gordon and they were messing about with me, acting the idiot.'

'Did you have any idea who it might be Ray?'

'None at all. I was there for a few days and it became something of a cat and mouse game. I even tried to catch whoever the joker was, but they always stayed one step ahead of me. Come to think of it there was one occasion when I did get a glimpse of someone disappearing into the hall. From the back, it looked like John, but it was odd because I was sure he was down the stairs. Anyway, it is probably not related, but I swear to God Gordon. The whole Deadwater House thing is strange. I know it is wrong, but I can't help feeling that the Denham-Grangers somehow had something to do with the death of my son.'

'That is rather a serious accusation Ray, what do you mean?'

Ray shrugged his shoulders wearily. I felt so sorry for him. 'I don't know Gordon. Maybe I am just clutching at straws. No parent should see their child die before them, it's just eating me up that's all.'

'Did you mention anything to the Denham-Grangers at the time Ray?'

'No, somehow I sensed it was not the right thing to ask, as though it would put them in an awkward situation, so I just finished the job and left. I did not think about it again until Steven started having his nightmares.'

'Ok Ray, well I will keep what you have told me in mind.' He went to get into his car and then stopped suddenly as if he had remembered something else.

'Oh yes, there was one final thing that day.'

'Yes, Ray, what is it?' I tried my best not to sound impatient even though by now I felt like lifting him into the car myself.

'I worked on the electrical wiring at Deadwater for two full days. When I left on the last day Roberta, John and the Housekeeper waved me away. I could clearly see someone watching me from one of the top windows. It was bizarre Gordon. I tell you those Denham-Grangers are hiding something, I just know it. The whole village reckons the same, they did something and it impacted my son. They have the blood of my child on their hands Gordon.' Ray started to get emotional, so I put my arms around him.

'I understand Ray, I know how tough this must be for you and Annie.'

With that Ray Warton shook my hand and got into his car. I stood and waved as he drove away. I desperately wanted to help him ease his pain but what could I do? Once he had disappeared around the corner I turned and hurried back into my cottage hoping to God that Imelda had not got bored and gone to investigate the outside toilet. She sat by the fire and looked up at me with that smile and those deep blue eyes. It crossed my mind how perfect she looked sitting there and how much I really was in love with her.

'Hi, Gordon, what was Ray here for? As I mentioned yesterday, I need to speak to you about something, it's about Steven so it's strange that Ray turned up as well'

'Jesus Imelda, if this is about ghosts or The Denham-Grangers then I need a fucking drink first. Ray was halfway through telling me his tale when you knocked, I damn near hit the roof. I thought this job was going to be missing cats and helping old ladies across the road, not the walking dead following me at every fucking turn.'

Imelda burst out laughing.

'You really are the limit PC Gordon Chisholme, how the hell did you ever end up as a policeman? Pour me a drink as well, I am going to bloody need it listening to you moaning you bloody big Nancy boy. You are supposed to be the tough guy, like Regan of The Sweeny on television, you are more like Sooty.'

'I don't remember Inspector Jack Regan having to chase fucking dead children's ghosts around, or maybe I missed that episode, Imelda?'

I poured two stiff whisky's out of my prized bottle of malt, one large double for me and a very small one for her. I should have guessed an Imelda move was about to come, it usually did and always took me by surprise. She reached out a grabbed the double glass and then sank it in one gulp before saying, 'By the way Constable Chisholme, I used your outside toilet while I was waiting for you to finish with Ray. Have you ever thought of cleaning that place up? It's fucking filthy.'

With that, we both burst out laughing. I drank my little whisky and poured us both another one, doubles for each of us this time. We settled down beside each other on the couch while Imelda told me her story. As expected, it was about the Denham-Grangers and Deadwater but somehow, I did not mind. I just enjoyed watching and listening to her talk. That is what being in love is all about I suppose.

Thoughts:

Can you picture yourself at 15? Surely this must be the hardest age of all, neither child nor adult. An air of violence pervades school life as boys seek to own their territory and girls try to rush towards womanhood. Parents become the enemy and friends become rivals. So, you search for everything that is wrong and grab it, no matter the consequences.

6

FOREVER?

(Deadwater House 1976)

Harry was bored, in fact, he was bored stiff. He had spent almost twelve months hiding inside Deadwater House. Although he could go outside on the days the gardener was not working in the grounds, he was still very much restricted by the confines of the Denham-Granger land and it was driving him crazy. He had set a target of one year staying completely out of sight and then hoped to slowly integrate back into the outside world while keeping his head down. The problem was, remaining low key did not fit with Harry's nature at all. The fear of being tracked down by the cartel he had double-crossed kept him in check for now but only just. He knew they would never forgive him, and his death sentence would stay until they either caught up with him or he continued to keep one step ahead of them.

Harry was reduced to making his own amusement as best he could. On one occasion he had toyed with the visiting electrician who John had called in to add mains electricity to the rooms Harry was living in. He had moved the guy's tools, poured beer into his tea mug and other childish pranks. The problem was that opportunities for even this limited kind of amusement proved to be few and far between. But it was not all bad, slowly but surely Harry had lured Roberta into his bed. He had always known his brother was gay, but he also knew that John would not accept him having an affair with his wife right under his nose. So, the clandestine meetings could only take place on one of the rare occasions that his elder sibling was either away in London or maybe out fishing his pond in the grounds of Deadwater House. The problem was Harry had even started to get bored with Roberta and was beginning to enjoy pushing things to the limit, almost as though he was taunting his brother to catch them out. He was also drinking, not a day would go past without at least one bottle of Scotch or vintage wine being procured from his brothers' collection.

Roberta was in turmoil. She had never fallen for a man, it had always been a business proposition rather than an emotional one when it came to boyfriends and even a husband. For the first time ever she was in love, she wanted Harry and she was sure he felt the same about her. *How could he not?* But John was the heir to the dwindling Denhan-Granger money as well as Deadwater House and Roberta would never give that up. She realised Harry would not be able to claim his share, that would require him showing face and being seen in public. If it ever became known that the younger Denham-Granger had returned it would certainly make the local press. Then it would not take long for his pursuers to put two and two together about what had happened to the double-crossing fraud they had known as Tony Brendon.

And of course, this Ménage a triose was always going to end in disaster and the day of reckoning arrived one early spring afternoon in 1976. It was one of those none descript days, the cloud cover hid the sun, but the rain was also kept in abeyance. It was almost as if the weather Gods had put everything on hold, so they too could watch over the unfolding drama about to envelop the imposing mansion of Deadwater.

John strolled across the grass towards the house, he had the air of a troubled man, unusual for the Denham-Granger heir. The last time he had felt like this had been 26 years previously when Harry had left, and he faced the prospect of having to take over the business from his father. The intervening years since meeting Roberta and his father's death had been perfect for John. Years of self-indulgence and doing very little, watched over by Roberta while she managed the house and looked after the finances.

How ironic then that the brother he had desperately wanted to stay was now the very person who on returning was threatening his very existence. As he walked up to the main door at the front of the imposing building John tried to convince himself that his inner turmoil was simply because he was annoyed. Maybe he was just angry with himself at having to walk back to the house for the fishing bate he had left behind when he arrived that morning at his favourite pond. And yet he knew it was far more than that. He had let his brother do whatever he wanted since returning but even the unconfrontational John could not ignore this one. *She is my bloody wife in the name of heaven. This is just one step too far Harry, you have gone over the line this time.* This was the day he had to confront his fears. Without admitting it to himself he had deliberately left the bait behind, so he could make an unexpected return to the house. The day had arrived, the day he would finally have to face up to his bullying younger brother.

Old Maud Stavely looked shocked when he walked through the door. 'Master John, oh we did not expect you back so early. Is something wrong?'

From the second that the old housekeeper spoke John knew his worse fears had been confirmed. Maud had gone pale and looked like a cornered rabbit caught in the headlights. He knew she would protect Roberta and lie for her even though it was really to look after him and the family name. Maud desperately wanted the status quo to survive and for Deadwater life to go on as it always had. She hated Harry as much as John did, but the circumstances had now dictated that she stop John from going upstairs at all costs.

'Where is the lady of the house Maud my dear?' Even in the deepest of crisis John still maintained the polite air of an eccentric country gentleman. It simply would not do to lose one's temper but inside he was burning up.

'John…err Master John, I, I, I am not sure I think she may have gone to the village.'

'Maud my dear her car is still here, you know as well as I do that Roberta does not walk anywhere. Can you please step aside and let me pass, if you would be so kind?'

John spoke the words in a measured tone as if for once he was having to try and keep control rather than being the control. Old Maud moved out of her employer's way, a resigned look of sadness scuttling across her cragged face. It was the end of the Denham-Granger era and she knew it. The fact that the whole antiquated set up had lasted into the mid-seventies was a miracle. Now rather than fade away like all the local gentry had, her charges were about to crash in an explosion that would finally start to see the ancient stones of Deadwater House crumble into the dust.

John calmly removed his coat and hung it on the stand as he edged passed the housekeeper. He took each step up the grand staircase slowly, making sure to make as little noise as possible. He walked tall, his head held high, the Master of the house no matter what happened next. The door into his younger brother's suite of rooms was not even locked, the brass handle turned smoothly without even a squeak. With a final deep intake of breath, John strode quickly towards the bedroom door and pushed it wide open. He looked upon the vision before him with disappointment rather than shock, maybe he had hoped it would not be true. For a split second, he saw Roberta naked and the strange thought crossed his mind that this was the first time he had ever seen his wife without her clothes on. Harry sat up and looked directly at him, nobody said anything. John closed the door and went back downstairs.

Roberta held both of John's hands in hers as they faced each other across the large fireplace. 'John, that is insane. You know Harry won't simply leave if you tell him to go. And then what happens next?' The people looking for him will have to do something about me and you. We will either be dead or end up losing everything. Even if all that stuff about gangsters is not true then Harry will still go through the courts to get his share. He will force us to sell all we have, Deadwater included. There has to be another way John, there must be.'

'He simply cannot stay Roby, no matter what you promise, I know him. He will work his way back in with you, the little bastard wants everything I have, even my bloody wife. In the name of heaven Roby, what are we to do.'

John was almost in tears, losing his constraint, emotion taking over for a rare occasion in his sheltered life.

'John, my love I told you, please believe me. Harry means nothing to me, the same as the men you visit in London mean nothing to you. It was simply for, well you know...sex. I just wanted to see what all the fuss was about.'

John looked in surprise at his wife, he had convinced himself over the years that Roberta new nothing about the real purpose of his visits to London. Even the mention of the word sex made them feel uncomfortable, two of the pampered rich still stuck in a time warp. Well at least John was, Roberta was a woman of the world. Her husband seemed more like a child and it had suited her for him to remain that way through the years. Cossetted by his name and his money, a life of gentleman's clubs, fishing and tinkering around with his heritage, Deadwater House. Roberta leaned forward to speak in a whisper to her husband as though the drunk and sleeping Harry might hear them despite being on the other side of the house.

'There is another way out of this mess John.'

'What is that Roberta?' John spoke as if he wanted to grasp at the solution his beloved wife was about to offer. She always came up with the answer to all his problems and he hoped that she was about to do the same again.

'We kill him, John. We get rid of him. No one knows he is here other than Maud. We pay her off and we get rid of him.'

John looked aghast at his wife. More so because he had expected her to come up with a solution and now she had lost the plot.

'Roberta, in the name of heaven, what are you talking about. As much as I would like the little rogue out of my life, I think you are going too far. Are you serious my dear?'

'Deadly serious John. I have never been more serious in my life.'

As she spoke the words John suddenly realised that Roberta did indeed mean what she was saying. He stared back at her in silence, his head in turmoil. But inside all that confusion crashing about his brain, there was a little thought that kept repeating itself...*Yes, if he is dead then everything can go back to the way it was. And who is going to know, who will ever find out? Once he is dead he is gone, gone for good. Out of our lives forever.*

***

(Witton Saint James 1980-83)

I sat at the little Police Office desk in late 1983 wondering how much longer I would have before they closed the village station down. No doubt I would be offered a move to the nearest big town, probably Ludlow. That would mean real shifts and having to work, something I was not particularly keen on. My mind wandered back to the last time I had seen Imelda, more than three years previously and yet still imprinted firmly in my memory. A lot had happened since then, life in the village was starting to change as more newcomers moved in. Don't get me wrong, even as late as 1983 Witton Saint James was still stuck in the past, but small changes had started and from then on, they would accelerate as the internet age dawned.

The evening Imelda came to see me a few years before had turned out to be both predictable and surprising. The part I expected was her continued belief that she and the three boys were being haunted by the ghost of the Denham-Granger child.

'Gordon, I know you think I am a crazy going on about this, but I swear to God, until I left the village and went to college, that thing followed me on at least three occasions.'

'Maybe it fancied you and wanted a date?' Imelda for once did not smile.

'So, you think it's a joke that Steven committed suicide then Gordon?'

'Sorry, Imelda. Look I know there is something in all this, but God knows what it is and really, what on earth do you think I can do about it anyway? I would be thrown out of the force if I started harassing the Denham-Grangers, they don't like me as it is.'

'Gordon, it has to be something to do with them. Why the hell did John Denham-Granger turn up at Steven's funeral? He knew nothing about him. There must be some link between him being there and us messing about at his house that day four years ago. It was as if he knew it was us and turned up to taunt me and Robbie.'

'Maybe the only reason he came was that he was drunk Imelda, I think he was taunting the whole village rather than just you. He only stayed five minutes and then staggered back out.'

Imelda went on to tell me that neither she nor Carl had seen anything of the ghost since leaving the village. She was convinced though that Steven was being haunted and that was part of the reason for the problems that led to him taking his own life.

'So, this thing, whatever it is, stays in the village? Well then unless it re-appears when you visit your mum and sisters surely the problem has gone away?'

'It's not just me Gordon. I caught up with Robbie when I came back for the funeral. He is acting odd. He used to worship me, now he does not want to talk. He seems so introverted now, as though he is scared. I am convinced it's the Denham-Granger curse. Seriously, Gordon, I am worried about him as well.'

I promised Imelda that I would have a chat with Robbie in the next few days and maybe take a run up to Deadwater House again. I was lying about the last bit, but I did intend to go and see Robbie. Between us, we polished off my one and only bottle of malt whisky that evening. It was not all ghosts and gloom as we laughed and chatted until late in the evening.

'I had better get you back to Little Steeping Farm Imelda, your mum will be worried about you, not to mention your boyfriend.'

'He went back to Birmingham after the funeral Gordon. Anyway, I would not say he is really my boyfriend.'

'Oh, what is he then, your fucking bodyguard?'

She laughed before replying. 'Maybe that is closer to the truth than you think. Anyway, PC Chisholme, what on earth has it got to do with you if he is my boyfriend or not. Are you jealous? You are I can tell, why has your face gone red?' She reached out for my hand and held it.

I will always remember that point as a defining moment in our relationship. We stared at each other without saying anything for a while. Her blue eyes challenging me, not even a blink. *Ask her to stay Gordon you idiot, go on ask before it is too late.* But like a fool, I started to feel embarrassed and could not say the words. Instead, I took the cowards option and stood up to break the spell.

'Right come on them Miss Poole, it is time I got you home.'

Was I imagining it, or did she look disappointed? She shrugged her shoulders and sighed before getting to her feet.

I walked her back to the farm feeling very drunk. Of course, the whisky seemed to have no impact on Imelda at all. She held my arm and laughed all the way back while walking in a perfectly straight line.

'Gordon, keep an eye to Robbie for me, promise me you will.'

'Yes, you know I will, Imelda, but only if you promise me one thing as well.'

'What is that then Constable Chisholme? Do you want me to bring you some dope back from Birmingham the next time I visit?' The words were said in that endearing Imelda style that I found so mesmerising.

'No, promise me that you won't wait another two years to come up and see me next time. Or at least come and say goodbye if your boyfriend proposes and you decide to move to Australia.'

She threw her head back and laughed, a sparkle in her eyes.

'Gordon, I have no fucking intention of marrying any dopey boy, and that includes you. Not that I would ever expect you to ask. Anyway, I am only 18, I intend to live my life and pushing a fucking pram is not part of it.'

'What makes you think I would want to marry you anyway Miss Poole? I have a line of girls sitting outside the police station every day waiting for me.'

'Yes, old Ma Capley and her sisters probably. I can just see you hand in hand with her walking down the aisle pushing her Zimmer frame in front of you.' The thought was both funny and repulsive. I gently pushed her with affection before replying.

'Well if Old Capley does drag me to the church then you had better turn up out of the blue to rescue me, Imelda.' She smiled back at me, her eyes melting my heart.

'Of course, I will Gordon. Someone would have to come and save you from yourself, that's for sure.'

Do you remember I mentioned the surprising part at the start of my reminiscing back to that evening?

Well, that came next when Imelda put her arms around me and pulled the two of us together before kissing me passionately on the lips. We stayed that way for a long time before she looked into my eyes and shook her head.

'That is a reminder PC Chisholme of what you could have had you big dope. I will be back to see you, Gordon, I promise.'

And with that, she turned and disappeared through the door of Little Steeping farm. That was the thing that I loved about Imelda. She never seemed to stick to any rules and was always one step ahead of me. While I was lying about going up to see the Denham-Grangers she was also lying about being back soon because as I sat there daydreaming in 1983 I had not seen her in three long years.

I did follow up on my promise to go and see Robbie a week or so later and my meeting with him was indeed troubling. The bright young boy I had spoken to in the past had been replaced by someone who looked tired and frightened. I visited him at Dom Stokely's garage, but he was extremely evasive and did not want to talk or answer any questions. I got a chance to have a quick chat with Dom himself and he told me that Robbie had indeed changed. He just seemed to want to stay at the garage and work, sometimes they had to virtually throw him out to get him to leave and go home. Yes, it was odd, but what was I to do?

Life in Witton Saint James was not all funerals and talk of dead children wandering the streets though. In 1981 they got me a little police car. It was an Austin Mini Metro, it even had a blue light and a feeble siren. When things got boring, which was pretty much most of the time, I would drive up to one of the derelict farms and fold the seats down to get a nap. It was bloody uncomfortable but after a few lunchtime pints at The Oak I could just about curl up and get some sleep. I was very rarely required to use it for any real Police business. Sometimes just for the hell of it I would put the siren and headlights on and race through the neighbouring villages pretending I was Starsky and Hutch. Of course, I did not do this in Witton Saint James as I would have been laughed out of the pub on a Friday night. The whole village knew damn well that catching criminals was not really part of my make-up. Mind you things were becoming harder and I had started to send out warnings to the locals that drink driving was no longer acceptable. I did issue a, *this is your last chance* out to a few of the old farmers but if I had taken it any further my name would have been mud in the village.

My quiet life as the local constable changed dramatically one early June afternoon in 1982. I think I was up at the old Maperley farm a mile outside the village having a snooze after a quick bite of lunch and a pint in The Oak. Suddenly a message on the police radio shook me out of my slumber. It was extremely rare for my police car number to be called out on the radio and at first, I thought I was mistaken. I sat forward in my seat to listen again and there it was, *Car 06 please attend a road traffic accident outside The Oak Public House in Witton Saint James.* I hammered down the hill to the village, blue light spinning and pathetic siren trying its best to sound important. I half expected to find one of the old farmers surveying the damage to their tractor after a few lunchtime pints. This was going to be difficult as I had been in the pub myself only an hour or so before.

As I rounded the corner into the village main street I saw the instantly recognisable yellow Cortina that Roberta Denham-Granger had been driving for several years. It was half embedded into the wall that protected The Oak car park, steam rising out of the crumpled bonnet. But it was not the car that grabbed my attention, no it was the staggering figure of the dishevelled John Denham-Granger in the middle of the road. A small group of regulars from the pub were standing on the pavement trying to talk some sense into him while also keeping their distance. I had heard that he occasionally arrived at The Oak to buy drink to take back to Deadwater. Usually, Roberta would be sitting outside, car engine running so neither of them would have to hang around. This time it looked like he was flying solo, or at least the car looked like it had attempted to fly.

Luckily my friend the young village doctor was on

hand, at least I knew he had not been drinking and would make some sense. 'What the fucks going on Chris?'

'Jesus Gordon, thank God you are here. It looks like Denham-Granger drove down to The Oak to buy whisky, I don't know why because he is totally pickled. Old Charlie Rook from the pub tried to stop him driving away as he could hardly stand. Looks like he almost knocked Charlie out then drove the car slap bang into the wall.'

'Is Charlie ok, Chris?'

'Yes, he's ok, although he wants a fight with Denham-Granger, in fact, all the locals do. Well, the ones who have been boozing that is.'

I looked over to the entourage of lunchtime drinkers standing on the pavement. Old Charlie was pulling his woollen jumper over his head as though he was getting stripped for a boxing match. The rest of the rabble were egging him on. It was ridiculous because Denham-Granger was a big man and he would eat Charlie alive in a fight.

'Just let me at im, oil fucking kill the posh fuckin bastud, just gives me a minute. Oil fucking moider im.' I turned to my friend with an air of resignation.

'For fuck sake, Chris. Can you do me a favour, get that lot back into the pub before old Charlie has a heart attack. I will look after Denham-Granger.'

Now, this was to prove a bit more difficult than I had expected. John Denham-Granger looked an absolute mess. It was hard to equate the raging drunk who faced me in the street with the easy-going Deadwater owner I had first met six years earlier.

'You try fucking touching me ya fucking copper bastard and al fucking mangle you into next year ya fucking piece of shit. Come on then, give me your best shot ya pile of crap.' By now I was in a stinking mood, it must have been the lunchtime pints and then being woken from my mid-day nap.

'Now look here Mister Denham-Granger. You are already in enough trouble without adding police assault to your problems. Come on John be reasonable. Get in my car and I will give you a lift home.'

'John? I will fuckin John you ya basturd. You are not even a proper fucking policeman. You are just another piece of village scum.'

I took this verbal assault as a hint that he was not going to throw his hands up in the air and say, *ok officer, you got me bang to rights, put on the cuffs.* Plus, he was starting to come towards me, spittle spraying out of his mouth in anger as he raged away like an angry bull. So, I did what I thought would be the next best thing. I sank my right boot between his legs and as he crumpled to the floor I rugby tackled him to the ground. Now look, I know nowadays this would be classed as Police brutality but give me a break, he was a lunatic, I had to think on my feet. Anyway, it seemed to please old Charlie Rook and his assembled pub cronies as they broke out into a round of applause. Chris came running over to help me lift John Denham-Granger into the Police car.

'Christ Gordon, that was a bit over the top. Could you not just have put the cuffs on him and been a bit gentler.'

'For fuck sake Chris, he is a frigging psycho. If I had not got him first he would have knocked me out. Anyway, he is village royalty, you don't stick handcuffs on the Denham-Grangers.' Chris tried not to laugh as he replied,

'Oh, good point Constable, much better to toe him in the nuts instead then.'

Chris helped me to carry him into the police car as we agreed the best thing to do was to get John back to Deadwater House. He was no trouble, I think the drink made him unconscious rather anything I had done to him.

I turned onto the drive up to the Denham-Granger house and could already see the figure of Roberta standing in the distance outside the imposing front door. It had only been two years since I had last seen her face to face. Now the change in her could not simply be put down to ageing. She would still only be 56 at that time but she looked awful. I had heard gossip in the village but seeing her was a shock. Roberta looked haggard, long gone was the attractive lady of the big house. It was only when she spoke that she sounded like the Mrs. Denham-Granger I knew.

'Gordon, I really do appreciate this. John has been having problems lately, he has been drinking too much. I do hope you can keep this out of official police business.'

'I will try Mrs. Denham-Granger, but you have to understand, a car smashed up in the village and a drunk man wanting to fight in the street is not something that is easy to hush up.'

She looked at me with a smile that held a hint of sarcasm.

'Well, I am sure that John is not the only one who likes a little drink before getting into a car. I am sure I have heard of others, why maybe even yourself Gordon. Let's just say this will be the last time it happens constable, you have my word for it.'

To be fair she kept her part of the bargain as the old yellow Cortina went to the scrapyard and was the last car that I was aware of the Denham-Grangers owning. John, as you might expect, never forgave me. From then on, I could sense his anger every time he was near me. I did hush the whole thing up but from that moment on I had to become stricter on the drink-driving rules. So, I stopped having my lunchtime pint and tried to keep away from The Oak at closing time to avoid having to get involved in needing to do any official police business.

Just after Christmas in 1982, I heard that Robbie had quit his job and left the village. There had been talk of him having mental health problems, so I was pleased to hear he had moved on. Maybe the supposed Deadwater house curse had been the reason but either way, I was glad for him and Imelda that he had left the past behind to find a new life. And so there I was, clearing away paperwork from my desk at the little police station in the late summer of 1983. I wondered where the last seven years had gone since I first opened the door as a rookie policeman when someone did open the door and walk in. Her hair was shorter this time although she still looked stunning but somehow her demeanour felt different. I could tell it was not going to be the social visit I had been dreaming of for the last three years.

'Hi Gordon, how are things with you? It's been a while.'

'Jesus Imelda, you know how to make an entrance. Why no contact for so long, you said last time you would be back soon. I missed you?'

'I am here for a reason Gordon, I heard Robbie left the village but that's not why I came back. Gordon, I am worried sick, I heard last week that Carl died in a car accident, Jesus, he was only 21 the same age as me. It's the curse, I know it is.'

She started to cry, it was the first time I had ever seen her lose control, she looked frightened.

'Gordon, what am I going to do, I can't sleep at night for thinking that it is coming to get me, please Gordon can't you do something. Go up to the house, find out if the rumour about the child is true. You are the only one I know who can get to the bottom of this.'

I walked over to comfort her and tried to put my arms around her, she seemed reluctant and stepped away.

'Ok Imelda, I agree. This has gone on for too long, I will do what I need to do to find out what is going on, hopefully, try to put your mind at ease.' She smiled at me, but those deep blue eyes looked at me differently, they no longer teased or goaded me the way they used to.

'Gordon, there is something you need to know.'

Somehow, I knew this was the part I dreaded hearing. I could have listened to stories of ghosts and Deadwater all day but not this.

'Remember I said it would never happen, well I got married last year to a lovely guy I met in Portugal. I fell for him and we just went for it. I am sorry Gordon.'

'Jesus Imelda, why are you telling me this? It's not as though we are close friends or anything. What you do with your life is nothing to do with me.'

I tried to act as though her words had not ripped me apart, attempted to be nonchalant and business-like.

'Leave the Deadwater thing with me and I promise I will do my best to get to the bottom of it. If you are heading back to Birmingham, then forward me an address and I will write if anything comes up.'

'I will be here for a few days staying at the farm with my mum. I am on my own as Claudio is working away, he knows the story but not about Carl's car accident. It would be nice to catch up with you Gordon, get a chat. We really never did get much time to piece all this together.' She still had that smile but now it had a hint of sadness mixed in with it.

'Sorry Imelda, I am busy, best if I get on with this Deadwater thing and treat it as police business.' I deliberately looked down at some fictitious piece of paperwork I was supposedly working on, trying to act as though her being married did not matter to me.

Of course, I was lying, I was desperate to see her but now she was married everything had changed. My dream that one day she would come back to the village and we would finally become an item was over. She looked at me with hurt in her eyes, Imelda knew as well as I did that I had always been in love with her. Without a word she turned and quietly closed the door and walked out of the police station.

I felt like a right shit treating her like that, but I was hurt, can you really blame me? To ease my guilt, I set about trying to track down information on what had happened to Carl. I knew that he had been attending university in Birmingham and used my contacts at Ludlow Police headquarters to trace the station that had dealt with his accident. The following day I got a call from Delilah Trapgear who worked in the Ludlow office. No, I swear to God, that was her real name. The poor woman had to put up with constant jokes from the male-dominated Police station, but she took it all in her stride. I reckoned Delilah had a fancy for me as she always tried hard to help when I requested anything. It was a pity she was married and over sixty though.

'Hello Witton Saint James Police station, Officer Gordon Chisholme speaking. Can I be of service?' I was messing around as I knew damn well it would be either a work colleague or a mate calling. No one phoned the village Police office on official business. Ok maybe old Ma Capley did but she had passed on and probably pestered the angels every day now instead.

'Ooh you sound so official PC Chisholme, yes I would love you to be of service.'

You see in those days even women could make sexual innuendo's and men would just laugh.

'No problem Delilah my darling, just name the

time and the place.' She chuckled before giving me the information I was looking for. Not only did I get the office I needed to contact, good old Delilah Trapgear even gave me the name of the officer that had dealt with Carl's accident.

'That's one you owe me young Gordon. I shall be waiting the next time you visit up here in Ludlow.'

I dialled the number I had been given and asked for Officer Andrew Benton. He told me that Carl and another young man had died when their car ran head-on into a wall. It seemed they had veered off the road just outside the university in Birmingham. Both victims were only 21, it was such a waste.

'Was there a reason they swerved Andrew? I mean was he speeding, or did they test him for drink driving?'

'No that was what was so sad Gordon. From what we could make out he was doing no more than 40 and no trace of alcohol was found in his blood. There was only one witness and she told us that the car just turned and drove straight into the wall. Neither of them was wearing seatbelts so the impact killed them outright.'

'Did you find any reason for Carl to swerve, I mean could it have been an animal or something?'

'Well it's funny you should ask because we did find some sort of slime on the road. Maybe it was from an animal, but we could not be sure.'

Within minutes of the phone conversation ending, I was heading to Little Steeping Farm. Hoping that Imelda had not already left to go back to wherever she and that new husband of hers were living. Just my luck it was her sister Michelle who answered the door. I had been out with her a few times, but she had ditched me because somehow, she got the impression that I fancied her sister more. She kept me standing at the door making it obvious that she held a grudge.

'Hello Gordon, what do you want?'

'Hi Michelle, how are you? Look it is official police business, I need to speak to Imelda. Is she still here?' The reply came back laced with sarcasm.

'Well is that not a surprise, you want to speak to Imelda! You are too late she has just left in a taxi to get the train to go back to her husband.' The word husband was emphasised at the end of her sentence. I tried to act nonchalant but as always, I did not know what to say.

'Oh ok. That's a pity. Oh well, maybe I can catch her next time. You will miss her Michelle now that she is married and gone for good?' Don't ask me why I said the last bit. I was never very good at ending awkward conversations. Michelle stared at me as though I was Satan himself before caustically replying.

'No, I won't miss her. There is only one thing

more boring than listening to you go on about her and that's having to listen to her go on about you. Why the fuck you two never just went out and gave us all a rest I will never know.' Then she slammed the door in my face.

I swerved the little police car around each bend, at some points, it almost reached more than 50mph. The feeble siren made a heroic attempt to clear the road for me. It always felt like cars moved out of the way in sympathy rather than anything else. Do you know how ridiculous it feels to be driving along in a marked police car with the siren and blue light going while a queue of cars follows behind wishing they could overtake? I screeched into Ludlow train station car park while praying that Imelda was not already on the train.

Someone once told me that in the seventies the old Nationalised British Railways only managed to run 5% of trains on time. It's fucking true and just my luck, Imelda Poole was on one of them.

Thoughts:

I loved being in my early twenties. I was at that age where you have no concern about the future and no guilt about the past. Sharing a flat with three friends, drinking, smoking and experimenting with different drugs. No mortgage, no children, no wish for a career, so every day becomes a Saturday. But all you really want is someone who loves you, and when you find that person the party must end.

7

A LADDER TO THE STARS

(Witton Saint James 1983)

It was about a week after Imelda had come to see me that I finally decided it was time I got off my backside and did something about the rumours and ghost stories. Well maybe that's what I would like you to think really happened, but it was not quite as straightforward as that. I was sitting in The Oak drowning my sorrows with my mate Doctor Chris Langton and another guy. I think his name was Barney but to be honest I am not sure. My memory can be rather suspect these days, maybe his name was Thomas. Anyway, this Barney guy was the son of a local village solicitor who had something to do with the Denham-Grangers. To cut a long story short it seemed that the hated couple of Deadwater House had gone away for a week for some reason. This was unheard of because in recent years they had hardly left the house. Maybe Roberta would go to the shops or John would crash his car into the pub every so often but most of the time they stayed at home.

'What's up then Gordon, you seem very quiet tonight? Usually, by Friday, you are desperate for a drink and some chat after a hard day solving crime in the village.' The question was delivered with more than a hint of sarcasm by Chris, he more than anyone knew I did very little.

'Nothing Chris, I am just feeling a bit fed up, to be honest. I think I need a change of career. I am getting bored wandering about doing the same thing over and over. Maybe I am just not cut out to be a Policeman.'

'So, I heard Imelda Poole was back in the village for a visit. A little bird tells me she went and got married.' Chris had a wry smile across his face as he said the words.

'Oh, Is she? I had not heard, how nice for her.' Chris tried not to laugh.

'For God's sake Gordon, pull yourself together man. You will start crying into your beer next. I know damn well you have lusted after her for the last five years, pretty much the whole village talks about you and Imelda Poole. She was always way out of your league anyway, far too good looking for a big lump like you. So, stop daydreaming and man up. Anyway, it's your round, I will have a pint, same again for me Romeo.'

It was hard not to laugh. I had not expected any sympathy and in fact, Chris was the most understanding, the others at the bar would rip me to shreds if they got the chance. The point is I had been in love with Imelda, or maybe a vision of her, Jesus I hardly knew her. I don't want you to get the impression that I would sit each evening writing poetry and feeling sorry for myself. I had been out with plenty of the village girls, one had even stretched to six months. Her name was June Lambley, nice girl but eventually, she told me I was too immature. June had no sense of humour as far as I was concerned. She got angry one day when I followed her in my little police motor. I put my siren on and pulled her car over for a laugh. She had not realised it was me and started crying as she was not insured. In fact, I don't even think June had passed her driving test. Being a gentleman, I let her off in the hope that she would throw herself at me in gratitude. She ditched me shortly afterwards, but on the plus side at least I did not have to do the paperwork for the charges. As you already know I had even gone out on a few dates with Michelle Poole, the younger sister of Imelda. The one who slammed the door in my face. Like her sibling, she was drop dead gorgeous, but I got a hint that she might have sussed me out when she said, *Why the fuck did you not just ask Imelda out, you mention her bloody name often enough?*

I stayed in the pub until closing time, even Chris and that Barney guy had gone home. I was absolutely hammered, but not enough apparently. I was the last to leave, even Bill Tavey the landlord was impressed enough to comment.

'Bloody hell Gordon, you have put away a few tonight. You even stayed longer than old farmer Davington and he prides himself on being last out. Take care of yourself heading up that road young man. Jesus, I bet you will have a sore head tomorrow, good job it's a Saturday and you are not working.'

As he closed the bolts over on the pub door I had a little chuckle to myself. *Fuckin am working tomorrow, forgot I have been asked to cover for the day up at Ludlow. Ah fuck it, I will be fine. Anyway, tonight is the night Gordon, tonight we sort out the Denham-Granger myth once and for all. I will show you, Imelda Poole, I will show you what real policing is all about. Fuck you and your fancy new poncey Latin lover'*

While talking to myself I lost balance and bounced off the little wooden bus shelter before tumbling forward head first into grassy patch alongside the path. I jumped to my feet, sobering up slightly at the thought of someone seeing me but need not have worried, it was pitch black by now. I brushed my jeans down and continued up to my little cottage. Within minutes I was back outside, a half bottle of whisky in my jacket pocket. Gloves and woollen hat covering the only remaining exposed parts of my body. I was finally ready for the raid on Deadwater House. It had to be now, the Denham-Grangers where away, I could not go up on official business as John hated my guts. I felt like an SAS commando going out on a highly secret mission. A very drunk commando that is.

I remember having an absolute bugger of a time getting through the forest leading up to the house. After around half an hour I finally reached the wall that separated the trees from the large lawn at the back of the imposing building. I was covered in scratches from brambles and a good few bruises having staggered into a tree or two.

Deadwater House stood like a large black shadow cast against the night sky as the moon made a pathetic attempt to shine through the clouds. I took a deep swig out of the whisky bottle and thought back to the story Imelda had told me about the visit with Steven, Carl and Robbie seven years previously. Suddenly it dawned on me that two of them were dead, one had run away, and one was terrified to come back to the village. *Maybe if it had not been for the Denham-Grangers and their fucking ghost child, Imelda might have lived on in the village and we would have got married, settled down, had kids.* The drink was making me lose track, that point where you are so drunk you think everything is possible. *I shall go up to the house, break in, find the body of the child and*

I will be a fucking hero in the newspapers. Imelda will ditch Carlos or whatever his fucking name is and come running back to me. Let's do this Gordon you fucking superstar, let's get this fucking sorted. I made to grasp the top of the wall and jump over, but my hand completely missed the edging stones. I went head over heels before landing with a thud face down on the Denham-Granger lawn. As I lifted my head I saw it, two greenish eyes staring at me about ten yards away. I scrambled in a panic to my feet and managed to leap back over the wall in one jump. Before fleeing I turned to look and see if the ghost was coming after me. I felt like a complete burk, a little fox could be seen silhouetted in the faint moonlight as it ran back off towards the house. I pulled the bottle out from inside my now muddy jacket and laughed while taking a large swig. The whole situation was ridiculous but for now, the whisky was driving me on.

Breaking into a house sounds easy but when you are confronted with thick doors and windows locked solidly against you it is a different story. The whole building was in darkness, not even an outside light was on. *Why the hell had I not brought a torch?* Even as I scolded myself I reached inside my jacket for the bottle. I took another large gulp while thinking up plan B. *Of course, that's it, never mind breaking in, check the sheds for a ladder and climb up to that window, use my lighter to see what's inside.* What was really happening was my bravado was wearing off and now my SAS raid had gone from housebreaking to messing about with a ladder. Job done, I could live with myself. *Anyway, what the hell did I owe Imelda? She had run off with Jose or whatever his fucking name was.* I was also starting to feel rather unwell.

You guessed it, the bloody shed was locked but nearby I did find an old wooden ladder half buried in the weeds and long grass. It may well have been the same one the kids had used, a few of the rungs looked dicey but it would do. It extended into three parts and after a lot of pissing around and cursing I finally got it up against the wall just below the little third-floor window. To be honest I was not even sure if this was the window Imelda had talked about but given the circumstances, I decided it would do. *In for a penny, in for a pound, one last swig of the bottle and I am up there.* Have you ever noticed how ladders don't look that high from the ground? And yet when you are at the top the ground looks fucking miles away. I nearly came off a few times but finally, I reached the summit, or as near the summit as I intended to get to. And that's when my problems really started.

Just as I was about to take the last few rungs and get a quick look in the window something caught my eye at the corner of the dark lawn. It was moving slowly around the far side of the house and heading in my direction. At first, I thought it must be the fox coming back to frighten the shit out of me again, but it seemed to be too tall, almost like a small stooped person. It was black, even blacker than the lawn, like a dead shadow. I could just vaguely make out its reflection against the grass as it glided slowly towards me. My body froze in fear, *what the fuck are you doing here Gordon, Oh God what if it's John Denham-Granger, he will have me drummed out of the force.* But it was not John Denham-Granger, it was something worse. I could smell it as it came towards me, it smelt like death, the same smell when I had helped pull Steven down from the rope he swung from at number 12. The same smell when I had broken the door down at Daisy cottage to find the decomposed body of the long dead Ma Capley. And then the worst bit came. It crept slowly to the bottom of the ladder and with me trapped at the top, it did the impossible. The filthy black mass started to climb rung by rung getting closer with every stinking breath. I took the only option I had left; no way was I waiting for it to reach me. I jumped, three fucking floors but I did it anyway. For a fraction of a second, I sailed into the dark night like a paratrooper and then nothing.

Imelda sat on the train staring out at the endless gloom of industrialisation that always seems to border railway lines as they enter the outskirts of large cities. Depressing graffiti and discarded crisp packets slithering along in the breeze. She thought about Carl and the letter she had received from his brother a few weeks back. He had not gone into any detail about the car accident but knowing he was dead was enough. Carl had been her first real boyfriend, a nice guy but it had not been a real relationship. Just two kids going out together. He had loved himself too much to really care about anyone else anyway. It made her depressed thinking about relationships, she was still only 21 and yet if she was honest she felt she had never really been in love. Various short-term relationships had ended as quickly as they had begun and now she was married. Claudio had swept her off her feet when they met on holiday in the Algarve just six months before. He was Portuguese, in his thirties but everyone said they made a beautiful couple, it had all just moved so fast. *Yes, why not, he is perfect. He is what I have been looking for, why wait?* Her mum had gone crazy, not because she did not like Claudio, it was just because she knew it was not real, a mistake. *He is too old for you Imelda and you are far too young to settle down yet.*

Imelda thought about Deadwater, it permeated her thoughts almost every day. She did not want to admit it, it felt too callous, unfair on Claudio and everyone else. How could she admit the truth, Imelda Poole had married because she could no longer face sleeping alone at night. She needed someone to protect her, hold her close in case it, the black thing, the child or whatever it was came calling. She could never risk being alone again, ever. She had only seen it when on her own in the village, never when anyone was with her. That was a comfort, but *what if it followed her, the way it must have done with Carl, the way it must have haunted poor Steven.* No if a loveless marriage meant she was safe then Imelda could accept that, and anyway, Claudio was a lovely guy, everyone said so. And then she pictured Constable Gordon Chisholme in her mind and smiled, a smile that made her feel uncomfortable. *Why are you thinking about that useless big idiot Imelda? You are a married woman now, he had his chance?* But no matter how much she tried to erase him from her memory she would still think back to the few times they had been together. And if truth be told she always did. What is it they say about never forgetting your first true love?

'Gordon in the name of Christ, what the hell happened to you. I saw you just before I left The Oak and you looked fine, drunk but, well bloody hell, Gordon.'

I could tell by the look on Chris's face that morning that I must have looked bad. I remember having a terrible headache and hoping it was just a hangover rather than something more serious. I knew my arm was broken though and my legs hurt like hell.

'I will have to take you to the hospital in Ludlow Gordon, your arm is broken, and God knows what else. Are you going to tell me what happened? Did you pick a fight with a Rhino on the way home last night?

'Yes, Chris, all in good time. Look, mate, I need a big favour, something you need to do for me before you take me to the hospital.

Chris gave me an odd look, a doctor and a police constable talking together but he knew something bad was coming next. 'What Gordon, what is it?'

'You need to hammer up to Deadwater House, get there before the Denham-Grangers get back. I left a ladder against the back wall, probably an empty half bottle of whisky and worse of all, I can't find my wallet with my ID card in it.'

***

(Deadwater House 1976)

For the first few weeks after being caught with Roberta the errant Harry tried to behave himself, pretend he was remorseful but, this could not last. It was now more than twelve months since he had gone into hiding and he was beginning to feel more confident, maybe the hunt for him had died down? Harry decided to head to London for a break, maybe it was a risk, but he desperately needed to get away from the claustrophobia of Deadwater. When Harry told his brother that he was leaving for a few weeks to see how things went, John was relieved. If his young brother would just go and not come back John promised, he would give him every penny he had

other than Deadwater House. But John was taken
aback by Roberta's anger when he told her about
Harry's plan.

'I don't understand Roberta, why would you want
him to stay? You promised me there was nothing
between you two anymore.'

'John, my dear love, how many more times do I
have to tell you. I hate Harry, he manipulated me. If
he goes to London I am terrified, he will get into
trouble and it will come back on us. You know him,
once he is free to do what he wants he will force us to
sell Deadwater, so he can have his share of the family
money.'

'So, what do we do Roberta, keep him holed up
here? I can't stand the sight of the little blighter, to
hell with him, let him go.

'It's a mistake, John, we should do what I said,
finish him now before anyone even knows he came
back.'

But John did not want to face the fact that the
problem would not go away. The thought of
murdering his brother could maybe have been the
solution to the mess they were in, but John simply
wanted to bury his head in the sand and hope Harry
would just disappear. John was not happy when
Roberta offered to drive Harry to the train station in
Ludlow. She had to convince her husband that this
was the only way if he would not agree to her initial

plan. When she returned John was relieved and some normality was resumed at Deadwater, at least until Harry came back. They both knew that he would return, it was just a matter of when and how much he was going to demand as his share of the Denham-Granger money.

Harry sat on the train heading for Crewe, one change and he would hit the heady delights of London at last. God how he missed the buzz of the city. Singapore to Hong Kong had been his run, he loved the thrill of easy money. He had known about the risks but then he needed the excitement even more than the money. Harry suddenly felt depressed, annoyed at his own greed and stupidity. *Why had he thrown it all away, the perfect lifestyle? Why did he ever think he could get the better of the cartel?* But his ego and natural bravado had convinced him that he could beat the men at the top, how wrong he had been. Now, something was needling him, telling him he was going to be wrong again, walking into another trap. But Harry could not stand the thought of another day stuck at Deadwater House, it was stifling him. *That stupid prick of a brother, lording about like a posh ponce and even worse, his pathetic wife. Yes, she had been useful in bed but give me a break, who the hell else was there. Anyway, she is well past her sell by date, I shall get me some young tart in London, spend a bit, live it up for a few weeks.*

Harry booked into The Churchill Hotel near Regents Park in Marylebone. It cost a fortune and was in some ways wasted on the erratic Denham-Granger. He immediately found a bar he liked and spent most of the day and evening there getting very drunk. He ingratiated himself with some of the locals by throwing his money around as well as trying to chat up every woman in the bar, single or not. On his third morning, the hotel manager woke him up by banging loudly on the door. Harry could not help but laugh when the stuck-up snob told him he had been caught urinating in the foyer on his return last night. He had also threatened and insulted some of the guests coming back from the theatre.

'I am afraid we will have to ask you to leave Mister Denham-Granger.' Harry gave the worried looking manager an evil glare and pretended to swing his arm back as though he was going to throw a punch. As the manager stepped back Harry laughed and slammed the door in his face. He packed his bag as quickly as possible and left before the staff called the police. As he walked down the road searching for another hotel a posh voice piped up behind him.

'John, John, it's me. How on earth are you old boy? Why its been positively ages since you came to London. Why did you not call me, we could have met up for old times' sake?'

Harry turned around to look at the well-dressed but old-fashioned gentleman standing before him.

'It's me Cedric, Cedric Townsend. Oh, come on

John old bean, stop kidding on that you don't recognise me.' Cedric went to squeeze Harry's cheek. It was obvious that the man facing him was gay and probably one of John's old lovers. Harry stepped back a few paces to make some personal space between them.

'I am sorry, but I have no idea who you are. Now best if you run along before you get me annoyed Cedric or whatever it is you like to call yourself.' But unfortunately, poor old Cedric did not take the hint and clearly had not realised who he was dealing with. He stepped forward to embrace Harry.

'Come here you old scoundrel, imagine not telling Cedric you would be in London. Surely you are not trying to dodge me old chap? Don't say you have gone and got yourself a younger model you absolute sneak?' Unlike the play acting, he had done with the hotel manager, this time the punch was for real. Cedric's nose burst open as the lights went out and he crashed to the ground. Within seconds his assailant was fleeing down the road.

Harry threw his case down and lay on the bed. The new hotel was only a street away from the one he had been thrown out of. It was not as upmarket but this being London, it was still expensive. He chuckled to himself as he thought back to the encounter with his brother's old lover Cedric. The incident was bothering him though. *Maybe I had better slow down, this was supposed to be a low-key visit. Better not cause too much of*

RICHARD M PEARSON

a rumpus, what if someone recognised me as Tony Brendon? It is not impossible, they could still be looking for me. Yes Harry, time to cool it a bit.

That evening he sat in the bar getting very drunk once more. An attractive young blonde girl seemed to be looking over at him, making furtive glances in his direction in between talking to her friend. Harry was now 48 but still carried that handsome rugged bad guy image with ease, or so he thought. Very soon Appoline was sitting beside him at the bar. She was in her early twenties and told Harry that she had moved over that year from France to work in the hotel across the road. The conversation drifted along until she said she had to go as she was working again in the morning. Harry did his best to impress her, desperately thinking up a plan to get the young woman into his bed. He begged her to come back to his hotel, have one last drink at the bar. Finally, she gave in, 'Ok, Monsieur Harry, mais juste un verre et ils doivent partir.'

'What, oh your French accent is just so sexy Appoline, you are going to tell me that means yes, surely?'

Appoline threw her head back and laughed, 'It Means, ok Harry but one drink and then I must leave.'

The couple walked out together, Harry trying desperately to keep in a straight line, pretend he was as sophisticated as the young French woman. Out in the street he turned towards her and whispered, 'You can stay in my room tonight if you want? Take the day off tomorrow. I can give you more money than you would earn in a year, tell the hotel to stuff it.'

Appoline looked at him with utter contempt and then in a broad English accent she replied, 'I have probably earned more money tonight in the five minutes it took to charm you than you will earn in a lifetime Mr. Brendon.'

Harry heard the crack as hard steel smashed into the back of his head with brute force and his body crumpled into the hands of the two men. Within seconds he had been bundled into the stolen Ford Sierra and it raced off down the street. Sarah meanwhile continued to walk down the road, *how fucking stupid men are. I mean Appoline, who the fuck has a name like that?* She felt her hand clutch the wad of notes in her coat pocket. Easy money, her very own thirty pieces of silver.

He woke up and at first thought he was either blind or dead. His head throbbed from the blow he had taken but other than that Harry knew he was ok and still alive for now. He could feel the blindfold around his eyes and the rope tied behind his back and looped through his legs. In the distance, the voices of two men could be heard talking but the sound was too far away to make out what they were saying. Instinct told Harry that his captors were not directly involved with the cartel. If they had of been he would either be in the middle of getting his fingers cut off while they forced him to talk or at best dead. *These guys must be paid hands, the cartel is far too professional to even think of leaving me alone in a room. They will be on their way, I still have time, think Harry, think.* He knew that once the real guys arrived he would be a dead man along with the two men chatting next door. No clues would be left, they would cancel him out, maybe torture him first to see who he had been staying with. Harry was already working his fingers towards the right-hand pocket of his jeans to get his lighter. *Christ these idiots did not even search me, they fucking deserve to die but I don't.* The pain of the lighter flame flickering against his wrist meant nothing to Harry, he had one chance to burn the rope and very little time.

Within minutes he was free and despite feeling dizzy he quickly searched the room for an exit. The back window looked out onto flats and small gardens strewn with refuse from the overflowing bins. He was two floors up, too high to jump but a drain pipe ran down from the side of the window. It was flimsy looking but his only chance. His senses picked up the silence, the two men had stopped talking in the other room. Within seconds he heard the commotion followed by horrendous screams, the sound of death. But Harry was already sliding and scrambling down the pipe. If he had needed to jump he would have, anything rather than face the born killers who had just arrived at the flat expecting to finally catch up with the long-lost Tony Brendon.

Harry was running, fleeing down the alleyways and side streets while laughing like a madman. His head still hurt, and his arms ached from both the lighter burns and the abrasions he had received while sliding down the drain pipe. But he was alive, no one had ever escaped the cartel and he had done it twice. They would never forgive him now, he would have to hide forever, and he knew of only one place he could do that. He slept rough that night in a London side alley, too risky to stay in a hotel and anyway they had taken his wallet if not his lighter. *One-night sleeping rough before that old Roberta picks me up after making a reverse charge call to Deadwater, why am I so fucking clever.* But even as he spoke the words in his head the thrill of escaping was being tempered with the thought of a life forever holed up in that house.

Roberta and John stood talking in the summer house, well away from any prying eyes from the imposing mansion facing them. The owners of Deadwater looked agitated, their conversation spiked with worry and emotion. Up on the second floor, Harry slept soundly while trying to recover from the excitement as well as the injuries from his London debacle. He had told Roberta nothing about what had happened other than to say he was in more trouble and would need to go into hiding again.

'We have no choice now John, someone will

eventually find out there is a third person staying here. I shall pay Maud off tomorrow, give her enough to keep quiet about Harry. She is loyal to the Denham-Granger name. It will be fine with her.'

John shuffled about uneasily, he hated all this confrontation and mess and he knew what was coming next from his wife.

'We have to kill him, John, get rid of him sooner rather than later. For God's sake will you listen to what I am telling you, John, if we don't we are all finished.'

She pulled the newspaper open and thrust the story into her husband's face.

'You know as well as I do John that this is something to do with him. Please in the name of heaven will you face up to what must be done, I can't do this myself.'

The supposed Master of Deadwater house looked again in horror at the headline in the paper. *Two men found mutilated in London flat thought to be gangland killings. Possible link with the body of a young woman found nearby.*

'But in heavens name Roberta, how do we do it? I can't shoot the little blighter, he is my brother in the name of God.'

Roberta showed her frustration and rising anger as she looked back at her husband. Then a thought came into her head.

'Ok, there is another possible way John. The back room up on the top floor, it was turned into a vault by your father. Leonard told me that the room was impregnable. That must mean that if you cannot get into it when it is locked, then you cannot get out of it either. If you can lure Harry up there, then we can lock him in behind the steel door. At least keep him in there until we can think of what to do next.'

Suddenly John realised the horror of what Roberta was suggesting but he was a coward, and this was a solution that would allow him to hide and not have to make a decision. Pretend the problem had gone away.

Within a few days, Harry was up and about. Roberta had let Maud go, the old ladies tears marking the end of a long line of Denham-Granger servants. Old Leonards concerns about the future of his business and the house being left in John's hands had all come true. Everything was either gone or falling down, soon maybe even Deadwater itself would crumble into the dust. The three remaining occupants seemed consumed in their own thoughts, almost as if each of them could not look the other in the face for the shame of what they had done or would soon have to do.

Roberta stood at the window and watched Maud get into her sons' car to disappear down the drive for the last time. She would miss the old lady who had been her loyal companion for the last 21 years, ever since she had first arrived at the house. Like old man

Denham-Granger, Maud had welcomed Roberta in the knowledge that she would control her hopeless husband John and then Deadwater House would survive when Leonard passed away. *Goodbye Maud, I shall miss you. But I know you will understand. You must go, it is nothing personal, it is simply a business decision.*

The imposing figure stepped gingerly into the vault on the top floor. Old bits of furniture littered the room, a thick layer of dust covering everything. No one had been in here for years, why would they? The Denham-Grangers no longer had money or valuables to hoard so the small room with the tiny single barred window had been allowed to rot along with the owner's name. Suddenly an arm holding a hammer flashed through the doorway but instead of striking the head of the man halfway into the vault it missed and crashed against his shoulder. He staggered back from the impact of the blow and turned around with shock to confront his assailant. But it was too late, the large steel door swung shut and even as he threw himself against it he heard the clunk of the key turning in the lock. And then the silence came as the cloak of Deadwater House wrapped itself around the prisoner as if to say, you belong to me now and death is the only way out.

Thoughts:

I found that in my twenties I went to a lot of weddings and then in my fifties a lot of funerals. In between would be the very occasional occurrence of either, usually when someone had got out of sync, maybe got married for the second time or dropped dead while running a 10k. You are going to think me terrible for saying this, but if forced to choose to have to attend one or the other, I would go for the funeral. They tend to pass far quicker, there is no dancing and I have yet to go to a funeral where they don't supply sausage rolls at the after service get together. So, you see, even getting to your fifties can have some positives.

8

DEATH OF A LADIES MAN

(Witton Saint James 1983)

Towards the end of 1983, I could sense that my time in the Police force was on shaky ground. After the fall following the drunken stunt up at Deadwater, I had been laid up for almost three months. The guy who had replaced the easy-going Sergeant Lawson as my boss was a different proposition altogether. I could tell that Sergeant Billy Raine or Billy the Bastard as he had been christened by the other constables in Ludlow did not trust me. I had concocted a half-arsed story about falling off a ladder while painting my cottage, but Billy the Bastard gave me that look as though to say, *I know you are lying Chisholme*. He could not do anything though as I was backed up by an official in Doctor Chris Langton, my good old drinking buddy. Don't get me wrong, Chris was not happy at being an accomplice in helping to cover my tracks at the Denham-Granger home. He made it plain that this would be the last time.

Billy the Bastard sent the worst possible replacement he could to cover my absence. Constable Garry Towse was a contemptible piece of work. New to the force and only 20 he was intent on doing everything exactly by the book. Maybe that would have been ok, but I kid you not, he had absolutely no sense of fun, none. He did not even enjoy charging about in the little police car with the feeble siren switched on. I could tell that the good people of Witton Saint James were desperate to see him go back to Ludlow. They would be as devastated as I was to learn that he would be staying until the end of the year to help me out. I somehow felt he had been asked to remain on in the hope he would catch me breaking the rules. Then he could go running back to Sergeant Bastard in the big town and they could kick me out once and for all.

The final nail in my long-term policing career looked to have come on my first full day back. Garry stood facing me at the little police office desk. 'I brought this from Ludlow head office Constable Chisholme, it's an official letter for you.'

'Look, Garry, surely to fuck you are not going to continue to call me Constable Chisholme every time we talk, it's getting on my fucking nerves. What is wrong with just calling me Gordon?'

'I think it is much better for our image as police officers in the village if we use our official title Constable Chisholme. If you have a problem with that we could always run it past the sergeant?'

I should have given him a look of either contempt or hatred but instead, I just felt resigned and tired. 'Ok Constable Towse, have it your fucking way.'

'Constable Chisholme, it might also be better for our image if you refrain from swearing as well. We are supposed to be professionals and your language really does leave a lot to be desired. I really do not understand why you have to use the F-word so much.'

I said nothing but was sure he could read my mind. *Fuck me, the first day back, I swear to God I will lamp this stupid big moron before the week is out.* As if things were not bad enough the letter was to tell me I was being given six months' notice of being transferred to Ludlow. The decision had been taken to close the Witton Saint James office for good from the end of May 1984. That would mean me having to work for a living and that went against everything I believed in. I could just imagine Sergeant Bastards face in Ludlow when I asked him,

'Hi Sarge, I have just had a few lunchtime pints. Would you mind if I take a kip in one of the cells rather than go out and pound the beat this afternoon?' or maybe, 'Good morning Mister Bastard,

I was wondering if it would be possible to get one of those American style siren's fitting to my Police car, so I can pretend I am a Texas Deputy?

I had only been back for a few days when the name Denham-Granger once again reared its ugly head. It was Chris who called to explain he had just been up at Deadwater house on an official visit.

'Hi Gordon, look I thought I had better let you know this although I don't think there is much you can do about it.'

'Yes, Chris go on. To be honest, anything you tell me would be good news. That new PC has got everyone in the village hating me. He spends half his time pulling up drink drivers leaving The Oak. At this rate, he will catch me next.' Chris laughed at my half-serious moaning.

'Well to be fair Gordon, maybe it was about time someone put their foot down before a really bad accident happens. Remember it will be me and you who will have to mop up afterward. Anyway, are you going to listen to what I have to tell you?'

'Yes Chris, fire away.'

'That is the third time I have been up at Deadwater this year, all for the same thing. Roberta looks terrible, lost so much weight. I can't believe how much she has aged.'

'Ok Chris, but come on, what has this to do with

police business or even me?' My tone was probably sharper than I had intended it to be.

'If you give me a chance I will tell you. God, you have been a right grump since the new PC arrived or maybe it's more to do with Imelda getting married?'

'Sorry Chris, yes go on, you were saying?'

'Well the thing is she is covered in bruises; a few times she has had sprained ankles or other injuries you might get from a fall. It is odd as it's only the two of them in the house now.'

'So basically, what you are saying Chris is that John Denham-Granger is beating his wife up? Let's be honest, who would be surprised, that lunatic has every other bad trait known to mankind. Why not add in a bit of domestic violence to his already colourful CV.' To my surprise, Chris answered as though he had doubts.

'Yes, it must be that. I suppose.'

We sat together like two big idiots jammed up in the little police Metro as we turned up onto the track leading to Deadwater House. In a way, I was looking forward to the outcome of this visit even though at the same time I was dreading it. Constable Garry Towse had insisted we make a cursory trip to see the Denham-Grangers after I told him what my friend Doctor Langton had said to me about Roberta. He had no idea what he was letting himself in for but no pleading from me would change the mind of PC Perfect. So, I decided to take a back seat and watch the fun unfold. The last time I have been up at the big house was to take the drunk John back after the accident more than a year ago. Even in this relatively short space of time the house and gardens had gone from unkempt to looking as though they had been abandoned completely. Bushes and overgrown tree branches scraped against the car as we progressed up the driveway. Even the once-manicured lawns were slowly disappearing into a sea of long grass that floated back and forth in the breeze.

Garry rapped on the wooden frame, a picture of confident authority with his dopey big pointed hat on while I stood a few yards behind. Roberta answered the door, well it looked like Roberta. She almost resembled a vagrant, someone who had been sleeping rough in the same clothes for the last few months. What had happened to the confident sophisticated woman I had first met eight years previously? She spoke as though she was no longer aware of her surroundings, just a body going through the motions of being alive. I could not see any flicker of recognition in her eyes when she noticed me standing behind Garry.

'Oh, it's the Police, how may I help you? Maybe I had better let my husband deal with this.'

It was as if she suddenly sensed that she must get John or there would be trouble. Only a few years before she would have dealt with everything but now they seemed to have switched roles and John had become the leader and Roberta the downtrodden follower.

'I think we would like to come inside if that is ok Mrs. Denham-Granger.' And with those few words, the pompous youngster simply walked into the house as Roberta disappeared into some far corner to find her husband. Inside the hall was strewn with leaves and scattered old newspapers, rubbish just left abandoned everywhere.

'Garry, I don't think this is a good idea, we have no real business marching into the house without a reason.' I just knew this would not turn out well but know it all PC Towse was having none of it.

'I think we have plenty of reason to be here Constable Chisholme, would you not say that wife beating is reason enough?' Now I know that most of you will think the spotless young PC Garry Towse was a hero for following up on the comment my friend Chris had made regarding Roberta. But let's put all this into a bit of perspective. This was still the early eighties and wrong though it was, unless you had cast iron proof and were willing to face the male-dominated courts of the time, few women ever got the opportunity to bring this sort of behaviour to light. But even worse, this was the Denham-Grangers of Deadwater House and as far as I was concerned PC Towse was about to find out what life in Witton

Saint James was all about.

It did not take long as within minutes John Denham-Granger appeared, a large man and a vision of pent-up fury. He too looked a mess and had the red bloated face of a habitual drinker.

'I told you to stay away Chisholme, you better have a damn good reason to come invading private property. Show me your fucking warrant and make it fast.' *Now that is bloody typical*, I thought to myself. *I am going to get the blame for that young idiot dragging me up here.* But divine intervention arrived when the young policeman stepped towards the large angry man facing him and announced,

'Mr. Denham-Granger, we believe you may have assaulted your wife and we are here to ask a few questions, that is all so please calm down.'

At that point the stooped Roberta who was standing in the shadows came forward. Suddenly she seemed like her old self and spoke with authority the way she used to when I first met her.

'Young man, I can quite assure you that my husband has never laid a finger on me. You have no right to make this kind of accusation, they are extremely upsetting for both of us. Could you please leave and…..'

She never got the chance to finish as John now had PC Trowse by the throat and was dragging him down onto the floor.

'You fucking little runt, I will fucking kill you. How dare you come into my home and make false accusations. I will kill the fucking both of you.'

Now at this rather difficult moment, I did consider just leaving my fellow policeman to sort out his own problems. Maybe nip down to The Oak for a few and come back later to scrape him off the carpet. But I suppose I felt sorry for him as well. I grabbed John and pulled his ample carcase off the stunned looking Garry.

'John, John, calm down, we are going, it's all been a mistake.'

'A fucking mistake, the only mistake around here is you Chisholme.'

Denham-Granger made as if to take a swing at me, but he must have still been pickled from drinking. The motion of pulling his arm back to make a punch meant his whole body staggered back and he collapsed into Roberta bringing the two of them crashing to the floor of the hallway. That was the perfect opportunity for me and the shocked Garry to take to our heels and run. We fled out the door and down the steps. It looked more like a scene out of the Carry-on Constable comedy although I am not sure which one of us was playing Hattie Jacques. Within seconds we were jammed back in the little police car and flying down the drive of Deadwater. I stopped at the exit back onto the B Road, still within distance of being able to see the house.

'Are you ok Garry? I tried to tell you that this was not a good idea. Denham-Granger is a grade one fucking lunatic. Has been for years.'

The white-faced and shaking young policeman looked at me, I thought for a minute he was going to start crying. It was hard not to laugh as he was still wearing his police helmet although now it was crushed down into his head.

'Yes Gordon, yes I am ok. Can we just get the fuck out of here please?'

'Please watch your language PC Towse, remember we are supposed to be respectable upholders of the law.' I think Gary was still in shock as he did not get the joke.

Of course, it was now compulsory for me to look back at Deadwater to see if the watcher was looking for us and as expected it was. In a corner window, I could clearly see the distant white face looking down at me.

'Ok Garry, just one last thing. Can you do me a favour and look at that window, third from the left on the second floor. Do you see someone watching us?' The still ashen-faced PC Towse looked up slowly and squinted his eyes through the dim sunlight. He looked at me with a look of bemusement on his face,

'What the fuck is that? Christ this place is weird, let's get the hell out of here.'

Garry only stayed on in Witton Saint James for a short time after the Deadwater debacle. I think he convinced Sergeant Bastard that I was doing a good job and there was no point in him remaining. In the last few weeks he was with me he seemed to lose his arrogance and turned out to be not so bad after all. He even came to The Oak one day after work for a beer and made the effort to ignore the local drink drivers for once. I decided against offering him a joint at the back of the police station or seeing if he wanted to put the car siren on and play Starsky and Hutch. Maybe it would have taken another few trips to meet John Denham-Granger again before he would be ready for that. I like to think that we parted as friends though and I felt I had at least left an impression on him when he commented,

'Take fucking care of yourself, Gordon.'

It was only a few months after the battle of Deadwater House as 1983 ended that three things happened almost at once. Three events that again stick in my memory, one sad, one odd and one totally unexpected. The first was when Chris walked into the little police station on a cold frosty morning between Christmas and New year.

'Hi Gordon, sorry did I wake you up?'

'Very funny, what is it you want Chris? Has

someone stolen your stethoscope?'

'I have some news for you. I have just been called up to the Denham-Grangers. Unfortunately, Roberta passed away last night. So sad, she was only 57 although she looked a lot older lately as you well know.'

'Jesus Chris, I can't say I am too surprised. What was the cause? Do you know?'

'Nothing suspicious Gordon, so don't worry you are not going to be asked to get involved. I know you and John Denham-Granger are not the best of friends. No, at the moment it looks like a heart attack, she was very frail.'

'I bet it was that shit of a husband that caused it though Chris?' There was a slight hesitation before my friend spoke again.

'That's the odd thing, Gordon. He seemed genuinely upset, I mean really upset, as though he really did care about her.' I gave Chris a look of surprise before replying.

'Jesus Chris don't tell me you feel sorry for him, he is an utter nut job. Anyway, even if he did care for her that still does not excuse him for beating up his wife.' Chris looked as though he was troubled and took a few seconds to answer.

'Yes, I know Gordon.' He sighed before going on. 'It's just that the whole thing is odd. Even though it must have been him that caused the bruises and injuries, somehow it does not stack up.'

'What do you mean Chris? What makes you have doubts?'

'I don't know Gordon. I wish I did but it's just a feeling I have, I can't put my finger on it.'

The second event I mentioned was the odd one. A few weeks before Roberta's death I had been in the process of locking up the police shed for the night. It was snowing heavily outside and the wind was whipping the white powder into a frenzy. It was hard to see more than a few yards through the blizzard. I bolted the front door and went into the back were the two small cells were situated. There was a rear exit that I would leave out of after picking up my jacket from the coat hanger beside the tiny prison. Suddenly I heard a loud bang and assuming it must be urgent police business I hurried back to the front office and unbolted the door. When I peered out into the storm there was nothing about, not a soul. I looked down at the ground and could make out footprints quite clearly in the deep snow. I stood and looked incredulously at the tracks, they came to the door and ended. The prints only came one way, it was as though whoever it was had arrived at the door and then disappeared. I finished locking up and then taking my torch I decided to follow the steps to see where they had originated from. Unfortunately, the wind was blowing the soft snow so hard that it became difficult to make them out after a while. I got as far as the edge of the village and the start of the track through the forest to Deadwater House before they disappeared. Somehow, I knew they would go that way. But it was not just the tracks that I remember, it was the smell. The same putrid stench that I recalled after climbing the ladder during the drunken visit to the Denham-Grangers property. So now I knew. The ghostly watcher from the house was finally after me as well.

And that is how 1983 ended, with me feeling depressed at the thought of leaving Witton Saint James the following year and somehow knowing that the Denham-Granger curse may well be true and now I too was a marked man. Whatever had been haunting the others had walked through the snow to find me as well. Oh, I nearly forgot, the third thing that happened, the totally unexpected one. I found a letter posted through my front door. Before I even opened it, I knew it was from Imelda, no doubt more bad news. I put it on the mantlepiece while I poured myself a beer and then when the excitement finally became too much I opened it. And you know what? Well, I already gave you a hint, the words were not what I expected, not what I expected at all. But that was Imelda for you, always one step ahead in taking me by surprise.

***

(Deadwater House 1976)

John Denham-Granger paced back and forward inside the small room. His shoulder ached from the blow he had taken, one that he knew had been aimed at his head. He was in trouble big trouble. John had already tried the large steel door several times, but it was locked solid. The only light in the room came from the little window and that could only open inwards as the iron bars covered it from the outside. He knew there could be no escape from the vault room. His father had it built to make entry or exit impossible to any potential housebreakers or even thieves amongst the once large staff. John could even remember the proud look on his father's face when the builders completed it in 1947, a few years after the end of the war. 'There will only be one key to this room John and I will hold it. Maybe if either you or Harry ever man up and take over from me then you can have the key to the family fortune.' Of course, within a few months, Leonard Denham-Granger had moved onto his next project and the room ended up being a simple store for old business records. Now it finally had a purpose, it had become the prison and maybe even the tomb for the Deadwater heir.

'Harry, Harry, get this door open, do you hear me. Look old chap this simply will not do, get this bloody door open now you absolute scoundrel.'

But no matter how much shouting or pleading he did the answer from behind the door was always the same, silence. Being imprisoned was not the only torment John had to deal with. He was worried sick about Roberta. The only conclusion he could come up with to explain what had happened was that Harry had overheard him and Roberta talking. *The little beggar must have listened in on us and then followed me when I came to check the vault. Oh God, what has he done to Roberta? If he has laid a finger on her I will bloody well have him.'* And then the reality of just how bad his situation might be dawned on John Denham-Granger. If Roberta was dead, then Harry could simply leave the house and he would starve to death in this prison. The housekeeper had been paid off and the gardener was on leave as well. Any other visitors such as the postman would use the front of the large mansion. But when John thought about it he knew that Harry could not leave as the cartel would find him. He also knew he could not stay at Deadwater if he murdered them both as surely someone would come calling and find out. *No, the blighter is just doing this to frighten us, probably has Roberta tied up downstairs. He will let me out, he must do.'* But somehow John knew his younger brother was capable of anything to save his own skin and each passing second in the vault started to feel like an eternity.

It was hard to work out just how long he had been in the room when John heard a voice from outside the steel door. Night had fallen, and it was pitch black. It had felt like days but was probably less than 24 hours. He was hungry and thirsty. *Thank God it is over. The blighter has taught me a lesson, he can stay if he wants so long as he lets me out of here. Oh, thank sweet Jesus for answering my prayers. But* the voice he heard shouting from the other side of the door was not Harry as he expected, it was Roberta. His precious love had come to rescue him. John felt a massive wave of relief, not only was he getting out of this awful room, but Roberta was alive and well too. *Maybe Harry had gone, left them to get back to normal and start enjoying Deadwater again.*

'John my darling, can you hear me?'

'Roberta, oh God Roberta, thank the Lord you are safe. Have you got the key, can you open this bloody door and get me out? I am so thirsty, I thought this nightmare would never end.'

'I am sorry John my love, I don't have the key. Your brother Harry is keeping it safe downstairs.'

'The little swine, ok Roberta, what does he want. Has he hurt you, my love? If he has I will bloody well be very annoyed. Have you tried asking him what it is he is after, what is it he wants?'

'Oh John, I thought that was obvious.' The tone of Roberta's voice had changed from caring to business like. 'He wants me, my dear, surely you must know that?'

John was confused, what on earth did she mean? 'What, what are you saying Roberta. He wants you? He can't have you, I thought you made it clear to him. What in heavens name is going on?' Panic was starting to appear in the normally docile John. He pressed his ear to the door and shouted, 'Roberta, Roberta, are you still there? Please, my darling explain. I am confused.'

'It is me he wants my darling and I have accepted his proposal. We shall leave for the Highlands of Scotland shortly for a few days. It is strictly business my dear, you do understand, don't you? I am sorry it must be this way but there is no other solution. If we don't do this then we will lose Deadwater House and you know that Leonard would have hated that.'

'Oh, Jesus Christ Roberta, what the hell are you talking about. How long do you intend to keep me trapped in here?' By now John's voice had reached a high-pitched screech as terror and panic took an even firmer grip on him.

'Oh, forever John my love, it will be forever. You can't come out and be seen again, that would simply ruin our plan'

'wh…wh..what plan Roberta, oh God what plan?'

'Oh John, you really are so sweet and innocent. Did you not see that I and Harry are in love? And you are the perfect solution. He looks exactly like you once he shaves his beard and puts on your clothes.

He can take your place, you will disappear and so will that Tony Brendon the cartel is looking for. It's so simple, Harry becomes you and we can go back to being happy and enjoy Deadwater again. Is that not what you always wanted?' John was crying now as he slid to the floor in despair, a completely broken man. He could no longer get any words out and was overwhelmed with the horror of his situation. And then he heard Roberta speak again, could it be an olive branch, could she show some mercy in his hour of desperation?

'John, there is one thing I want to tell you, it might help you.' John's head lifted from the ground, the condemned man hoping to be given a last-minute reprieve. 'Yes Roberta, yes, what is it, go on.'

'Your father would have been so proud of the solution we came up with to save the Denham-Granger name. You should be so happy John. At last, you have done the right thing for the family, for Deadwater. How fitting that old Leonard built this room, so Harry could come back and take over.' She chuckled to herself before saying her final words.

'Take care my love and remember, please do not think poorly of me, this was after all just simply a necessary business decision.'

John started to regain consciousness again. He had drifted in and out over the last few days as the ravages of having no food and water took over. In the early days, he had searched the room, learning the survival instincts that had totally eluded him in his cosseted life as the Master of Deadwater. For the first time in 52 years, he had to work out things for himself. He found an old discarded bowl amongst the musty paperwork and books and devised a way of holding it between the bars of the little window to gather rainwater. The problem was it did not rain long enough to give him the amount of the vital liquid he needed. It did help though, and he also found some nourishment in the spiders and other insects that infested the long-forgotten room. But after a few weeks, he was falling apart as the ravages of starvation took over.

As he opened his red blistered eyes one-morning bright sunlight once again peered through the little window. And then he heard the noise, was he dreaming, hallucinating again? Without moving his body, he managed to turn his head and focus on the opening. Something was appearing at the bottom edge of the window. *This was impossible, it looked like the top of a ladder.* John was already forcing himself to his feet, the pathetic last act of a dying man. He hobbled inch by inch towards the window and then he saw the hand push the frame inwards and reach in. In a last desperate act, he grabbed at the arm and croaked out what would be his final words. *'Water, water, please, oh God please get me water.* But the arm had already disappeared, and John's last ounce of strength slipped away as he once again fell to the floor of his prison.

Harry steered the Yellow Cortina into the drive. He looked nervous and so did Roberta. Harry was a hard man, he had killed before and thought nothing of it. This was different, he had left his brother imprisoned for nearly two weeks. He hoped to God his sibling was long dead and they could bury the body. Harry could not stand the thought that John might still be alive when he unlocked the vault. Roberta continued to try and convince herself that this had all been necessary. If she had not followed through with the plan, then they would have lost Deadwater and possibly all three of them would be dead in the long run. The fact that Harry looked so much like his brother was perfect. John had hardly been away from Deadwater in years and so long as the imposter Harry played the game, then they could pull this off. *You had no choice Roberta, it had to be this way. Surely even John could understand the need for him to be the sacrifice to save the family name?* As the car inched around the side of the house a look of horror crossed Roberta's face.

'Oh Jesus Harry, look someone is on a ladder up at the back window, it looks like two boys. It's those little toe rags from the village.'

Harry was already out of the car, in a blind rage, *how dare they the little bastards*. But he was no longer a young man and even though he almost got a hand on one of them they proved to be too fast. He continued the chase until they vaulted the wall and fled into the forest. *Surely, they can't have seen anything, John must be long dead by now? But why the fuck were they trying to get up to the window anyway?* He pulled up gasping for breath as he reached the trees that bordered the Denham-Granger land. He was sure he could make out more than two figures disappearing into the thick wood.

They agreed between them that Roberta should go to the police station and report the attempted break-in. That way it would hopefully show they had nothing to hide. Harry felt it would be unlikely that the boys had seen John's body, but it was a worry. The last thing they needed was some country bumpkin policeman nosing around. This left Harry with the unenviable task of opening the vault to check the remains of his brother. He intended to wrap him in a large blanket and then drag the body out to a ditch he had started digging outside near one of the garden sheds.

Harry crept gingerly up to the door and pressed his ear against the cold steel. As expected all was silent so he slowly inserted the key and pushed it open. The stench nearly knocked him off his feet, this was something he had not thought about. When he had murdered his adversaries in the past it had been easy. Kill and run, but this was different. In the dim room, he could make out the pathetic body of his brother sprawled face down by the little window. For the first time in his life, Harry felt some pity and remorse at what he had done. *For fuck sake, pull yourself together Harry, it's only a dead body. Let's get this over with.'* Harry strode over towards his brother with a fake confidence he did not feel. He peered down at the back of John's head and then jumped back startled. He could have sworn the body had moved. *Maybe you can survive without food and water for two weeks?* Harry went downstairs and came back with the hammer he kept in the kitchen. *Sorry John but this must be finished, you should be dead by now for fuck sake.* He stood over his brother and went to raise the mallet in his hand. Johns bony arm grabbed his ankle and Harry fell screaming to the floor in shock, the hammer falling with a thud to the ground. Harry sat looking in horror as the skeleton like figure of his brother crawled towards him. Once more it made a pathetic attempt to grab at his leg and stop him escaping out of the door. For the first time in his life, Harry was genuinely terrified. He staggered to his feet and edged back to the steel frame while the skull of his sibling stared at him. Harry slammed the door shut and turned the key, sweat running down his forehead and his eyes wide with fear.

And that would be the last time for many years that Harry or Roberta Denham-Granger would open the door to the vault again. The only way they could cope with the horror they had committed on an innocent man was to simply wipe it from their memory and let it fade away through time. Well maybe that is what they hoped would happen but if life is never easy then neither is death. They might not have felt so protected by the mass of solid steel that Leonard Denham-Granger had watched being installed with such pride if they had seen the final act of the dying man on the other side of it. Even as Harry stood panting pressed against the door, the body of his brother had shuffled grotesquely to its feet. Hatred and retribution seeping from every pore of his dead decaying skin. At long last Leonard, Harry and Roberta had turned the gentle John Denham-Granger into something he could never be in life. But now that he was dead it was going to be so different. Now he could seek revenge, now he would make them all pay with their lives. But firstly, they and everyone else would suffer horribly for every second he had been imprisoned inside the vault.

Thoughts:

My father when he was young used to be an amateur boxer. I was told by my grandfather that he was good and won many medals. When I was growing up it was hard to equate the respected businessman I was in awe of with a brutal boxing ring. I reckon that in his day fighting for sport was how you learned to survive. One day I went to visit him in the care home only months before Alzheimer's consumed his brain. The male nurse took me aside and told me my dad had got into the Queensbury rules stance against him as though he was in a boxing match again. I suppose that in a way to him it was a fight. I know it is wrong to say it, but I felt so proud of him that day.

9

THE DEAR JOHN LETTER

(Witton Saint James 1984)

I know you are probably thinking, *tell me what was in the letter from Imelda?* Well, it was addressed to me rather than you, so I am under no obligation to let you see it. But as you have stuck with my tale this far I will get to it. First things first though, we both have a funeral to attend.

The memorial for Roberta was held over until early 1984. I arrived once again at Saint John's on The Mound church in full uniform. I remember thinking this might be the last one as once I was transferred to Ludlow it would no longer be expected or even practical to attend every Witton Saint James funeral. This one was going to be different though, for a start it was the internment of village royalty even if it was hated village royalty. A big crowd was expected and judging by the cars arriving I was not going to be disappointed. A few had come to pay their respects to Roberta, maybe a handful from her past life in London. Most had come in the hope they might catch a glimpse of the reclusive drunk John Denham-Granger. The order of service clearly stated that there would be no get together after the funeral. I was not surprised as I knew John would not want to talk to anyone but like most, I had been hoping for a free lunch afterwards. It seemed the least the bereaved family could do was supply the guests with sausage rolls and egg mayonnaise sandwiches for turning up, but it was not to be. You could sense the air of disapproval amongst the locals. I could imagine the pub gossip Paul Davington mumbling away to old Rosie Davington back in the fifth row of the church.

Thems that's got money is thems that aint willin to spend it. Nevur liked them Denham-Grangers and shows I was right, not even a bloody sausage roll. And us in the village what gave them such respect. Allurs tights wif their money the big ouse uns. Not a fuckin sausage roll, nowt. Old Rosie would no doubt shake her head in agreement before sinking the boot in as well.

Kept tur money for themsels they did. That Roberta was a wrong un for sure, thought she was above us poor villagers, and now not even a bloody sausage roll. Flouncin around the village lordin it over us and they can't even give us a cup o tea. And us what has got dressed up to pay ower respects as well.

As many as 200 people crammed into the little

village church. Most of them would be squinting around to see how the other women had dressed for the occasion so they could gossip. *That is typical of that old skinflint Rosie, she wears the same dress to every funeral. I am sure she wore that outfit to Leonard's service in 1957.* Or, *will you look at Trudy Poole, she must have borrowed that skirt from one of her daughters, it is far too short for a woman in her fifties.* Most of the men would nod in agreement while quietly thinking, not long now and we can get a pint in The Oak.

The Minister was already well into his speech when an audible gasp could be heard from the assembled congregation. The man we knew as John Denham-Granger had shuffled in helped by a middle-aged companion who we assumed was his lawyer. Even in the few months since the unfortunate visit with Constable Towse his decline had been rapid. Most of the villagers had not seen him in years so to many of them the sight of the old and haggard looking master of Deadwater was a shock. It did not help when the fashionable country gentleman of old was dressed in an old coat and woollen hat that made him look like a tramp. A scruffy white beard covered most of his face and matted filthy strands of hair hung down over his shoulder. He walked, or should I say hobbled along with a walking cane.

Once the service was over the congregation rapidly dispersed. No doubt most would be disappointed at John Denham-Granger not rising to the occasion and disgracing himself as he had done in the past. Personally, I was still thinking about the missing sausage rolls, so it came as a surprise when the lawyer looking chap called me over. 'Constable Chisholme, my name is Henry Mollet-Lambton, may I have a word please?'

'Yes, Sir, how may I help you?' He took my hand and shook it vigorously.

'My client Mr. John Denham-Granger has asked if you would mind driving him back to Deadwater House? He tells me you are the only person in the village he respects and would like to have a chat about something.'

As you would expect, I knew the bit about him respecting me was bullshit. The Denham-Granger I had come to know hated me even more than the rest of the village, so something was going on. Not only that, I was scared stiff of him. Without being too blunt, as far as I was concerned he was an uncontrollable fruitcake.

'Are you sure he would not rather you took him home Mister…sorry what was your name again?'

The lawyer insisted that Denham-Granger wanted me to run him back so, in the end, I had no choice. I walked over with the esteemed Mr. Mollet-Lambton to the Bentley that he had arrived in and opened the door with trepidation.

'Mister Denham-Granger, may I offer my sincere condolences regarding the loss of your wife Roberta. She was such a lovely woman. My car is just over there if you would like a lift back to Deadwater?' I suppose I was nervous as I stood pointing at my car like an idiot.

'Are you trying to be funny Chisholme, I know what one is your fucking car when it has the word Police in great big fucking letters plastered down the side of it.' Once again, I had not got off to the best of starts with the big madman, but he just seemed to have that effect on me. Somehow, I knew this was going to be a very uncomfortable journey back to his mansion.

The ride from the village to Deadwater took about ten minutes, we drove in silence although I could feel the tension between us. Mine felt like nervousness, his was hatred. On arrival at the big house, I waited patiently for him to get out of the car, but he sat there and fidgeted with his hands.

'Is there something you want to say Mister Denham-Granger?' He turned slowly and looked at me. Anger written across his prematurely lined face.

'What is it that you and the rest of the scum in the village want from me?'

'I don't understand Mister Denham-Granger, what is it you want me to say?'

'You know fucking well what I mean Chisholme. You have been at my property a good few times. in fact, you had the audacity on your last visit to accuse me of beating Roberta up.'

I sensed he was not getting to the point he really wanted to make. 'Look, John, most of the times I have been here it has been just a friendly visit or to drop you off after you crashed your car in the village. I am sorry about the last time but that was PC Trowse and I had no authority to stop him. I told him you would go craz.....be annoyed but you know what these youngsters are like.'

His face went red with anger while I sat uncomfortably in my seat wondering what I had done wrong now. 'Don't fucking call me John you officious big prick Chisholme.' He spat the words out at me so hard that drops of spittle ran from the corners of his mouth.

'What the fuck is it you and those slimy bastards in the village really want? Go on tell me why you sent those kids up that day and why you and others come to my house uninvited? Someone was at it again last year, that same old ladder had been moved, marks on the grass. Don't fucking lie to me Chisholme.'

By now he was starting to get into a rage and I panicked, said the wrong thing but I was shit scared. He was a big man, and this was a confined space. We were wedged into the little motor car like two sardines. Ok, the last time I had kicked him in the nuts, but he was drunk then, it had been easy. I half expected him to pull out a knife, the man was fucking loopy. The words were out before I could stop,

'The villagers think you murdered your child and kept the body hidden in the house, it's crazy I know but that's the daft story they have in their heads. Of course, I realise it is a lot of nonsense but that's what they believe.'

I went to grab the handle and get the hell out of the little police car before he flipped, but Denham-Grangers reaction was not what I expected. He was laughing, the demented cackling of a man who has gone over the edge. He pulled the catch of the door and stepped out of the car leaving me looking both relieved and bemused.

'A fucking child, hahahahahaha, a child, yes maybe you lot are not so crazy after all, but Jesus Fucking Christ, a child, hahahahahaha.'

As he disappeared into the run-down mansion I sat and pondered on his words. They left me in a difficult situation. He was clearly taunting me, almost admitting that something had happened at Deadwater House. But what could I do? I had no evidence of him doing anything untoward and if I tried to follow up he would no doubt say I was continuing to harass him.

I drove onto the empty B Road back to the village

lost in my thoughts. Trying to pull all this weirdness into some logic, some reason. *What had happened back at the mansion, what had Denham-Granger done to cause all this heartache and fear?*

Christ, the black figure stood in the middle of the road facing me. In a panic, I pulled the steering wheel sharply to the left in a desperate attempt to avoid a head-on collision. Just before the sickening thud of metal upon flesh, I could see the face of the man I had just left. Only this time John Denham-Granger looked dead, emaciated and filthy like a walking corpse. The car screeched towards the ditch and bushes at the side of the road before somersaulting onto its roof while I bounced around inside like a pinball. It finally came to rest facing back onto the road but upside down. Incredibly I was still alive and being held in position by the seat belt. I ran my hand over the various parts of my body to make sure nothing was missing or damaged. Everything seemed ok with me but the same could not be said of the little police car. The windscreen had shattered into tiny fragments of glass while the steering wheel and dashboard lay at an odd angle. Wires and bits of crumpled metal surrounded me. You are going to think this is strange but rather than make a hasty retreat out of the wreckage do you know what I did next? My hand reached down to the broken panel and I flicked the switch marked SIREN on. And then I burst out laughing as it made the same pathetic attempt to sound important, just for one very last time. I released the belt and crumpled into the roof before scrambling out through the driver's window and looked myself over. Other than mud and grass stains I was unscathed. The same could not be said of my little metal companion. Steam hissed out from the upturned chassis and black pools of oil were forming beneath it. The car was beyond help and I knew this would not go down well with Sergeant Bastard. The apparition was no longer around, if it had ever been there in the first place.

I walked out into the middle of the tarmac to the place where the ghost had been standing. Of course, the tell-tale slime marks could clearly be seen making a track back to the woods that surrounded me. Luckily a motor came along the usually quiet B Road within five minutes and pulled over to offer me a lift. Just my luck it turned out to be Trudy Poole, Imelda's mother. I had the feeling she liked me, but I could tell she was thinking, *Gordon, such a nice big guy but God help us if that's who they let into the police force these days*. It would be hard not to blame her; my reputation was poor even before I wrote off the car. She dropped me at the police station, 'Are you sure you are not hurt Gordon?'

'No, I am fine Mrs. Poole, just my pride. Tell Imelda I was asking for her next time you see her.'

'Well she has moved a long way from the village Gordon and has a husband now, so I don't suppose she will be back much.'

I could tell what she really wanted to say was, *forget it, Gordon, she is married to a successful handsome businessman from Portugal. Thank the Lord she did not end up with you.*

I was in big trouble. It had only been a matter of months since I had returned to work after my fall off the ladder. Now I had to phone Ludlow headquarters and tell them their police motor had lost a fight with the ghost of Deadwater and was upside down in a ditch. I came up with some half-hearted story about skidding on mud, but it was obvious that I was lying. Sergeant Bastard turned up that afternoon at my cottage with an Inspector. He told me I was suspended from duty pending investigation of the accident by the traffic police. I knew I was done for but to be honest I was ready to quit anyway. Maybe this just made it easier for me although my mum was probably going to kill me. Funny how even at 28 guys are still scared of their mothers. To say I had reached a low point in my life would have been putting it mildly. My career was in ruins, the curse was now on my trail and worse of all Imelda was gone for good. Life was not exactly dealing me a Royal Flush as they say.

Oh yes, I almost forgot, the letter…

Dear Gordon,

I thought it best to write to you as for now I have no intention of returning to Witton Saint James and I suppose we may never meet again. Claudio's work will take him to Edinburgh for the next few years, so we have rented a lovely house in a place called Haddington to allow him to commute to his office. We never really got a chance to talk in the summer when I came to see you. I was sad that you seemed so short with me, but I know why Gordon. I am not an idiot; the whole village jokes about you having a crush on me. I hope I have not made your face go read while you read this, I have haven't I. You really are a big dafty PC Chisholme.

I am sure the village gossips have told you that Claudio is older than me, well 14 years to be precise as he is 36. He is a lovely guy and to be honest Gordon I needed someone to look after me, keep me safe at night. I am still convinced that the Denham-Granger child is haunting me and the rest of the gang. Both Carl and Steven are dead and the last I heard of Robbie he had left the village but was having mental health issues. I spoke to his father on the phone a few months back and he told me Robbie is in care, it is just awful.

I know you think I am crazy Gordon, but I have seen that apparition at least four times over the years, sometimes I feel it even watches me from a distance. So far it has not followed me out of the village, but I know it will find me one day. Maybe that is why I rushed into marriage, I hate being alone, what if it came to me in the night? So, I make sure to have someone around all the time. Am I insane Gordon? Maybe I am but either way, it is a curse and I am terrified of what will happen. I realise your hands are tied regarding Deadwater House but somehow, I feel that this could be solved if whatever it is can be laid to rest. The only way to do that? Get into the Denham-Granger home and find out the truth.

Anyway, enough of my moaning. I really do hope you find happiness PC Chisholme. Somehow, I don't think you will stay in the police, the word in the village is that you could end up being drummed out. What will you do? Maybe it would be the best thing for you, get a real job and find that girl you want to marry. I was thinking the other day about that time we kissed after Stevens funeral. Maybe if things had been different and Deadwater did not watch over us all, well maybe it would have been easier for me and you?

Well, I shall go now. I think it best if you do not write so I will not supply my address. I also want to break all ties with the past as much as possible. So, there is just one last thing to say. I think I knew you were in love with me, I could see it in your eyes. Well you big idiot, I hope you learn from this because even though I would not admit it to myself, all I ever really wanted was for you to ask me out. You never did.

You see Gordon Chisholme, I think I was as much in love with you as you were with me.

Imelda Poole. (December 1983) XXX

***

Deadwater House (1976-1984)

The first six months of Harry and Roberta having the house to themselves passed peacefully enough. The couple had talked over their plan meticulously during the two weeks in Scotland. Harry was to assume Johns identity and Roberta would school him to make a passable impression of her former husband. She knew Harry was a hothead but tried her best to calm him down. The fact that he had escaped the clutches of his previous employers and survived made him realise he now had no choice but to make this a success. He had been given a second chance and if he screwed this up he would not get another. The painful death he and Roberta had inflicted on John also played on his mind far more than any previous murders he had been involved in. Harry also knew that he could not screw Roberta over either as both now held equal power with each other. If truth be told he started to almost admire her, the old bird was not so bad after all. *Maybe once things settle down I can do this John Denham-Granger impersonation and start getting out and about again.* And so, the new couple of Deadwater almost fell into normality, Harry would drink too much and get rowdy but usually, he would fall asleep. Roberta would stay close to the house to make sure he behaved although she was at least starting to get out to the nearby town again. Sometimes even Harry would come with her and they would play act their role as the happy middle-aged couple. Of course, they never discussed the room or even went near it if possible. The vault and its rotting contents remained tightly locked.

And maybe they would have embraced an unlikely old age together if things had remained that way. Perhaps Roberta could have kept Harry's fiery temper under control and they might have pulled the whole thing off. But it was not to be, because even as they started to push the vault to the back of their minds things inside the room were changing. Death had awoken from its slumber and was about to walk the halls of Deadwater House as well as the village of Witton Saint James.

It was not long after Christmas 1977 that the Denham-Grangers got their first hint of what was to come. Outside the large house, the snow swirled as the winter wind howled through the trees. It was late afternoon and already Harry was nodding off having consumed more than a few of the bottles of wine his brother had collected in the cellar downstairs. Roberta watched him with a frown, it was catch 22, drink seemed to mellow Harry but often he would have too much and fall asleep. Her ears pricked up as she heard a low moan almost like the sound of the wind but somehow not quite. She was nice and warm sitting beside the large fire although it had become a nuisance having to make it up each day themselves. *If things remain calm for another month or so maybe we can think about getting a new housemaid, this place is too big for me. I am sure the money would stretch to cover it, maybe even sell some more of the furniture and paintings.*

Roberta's thoughts were once again interrupted by a low moaning sound. There could be little doubt now that it was coming from one of the two floors above. *It must be the wind,* she thought to herself, but something was making her feel uncomfortable. 'Harry, Harry, wake up, do you hear that noise, oh for heaven's sake wake up will you.' Roberta had always insisted that she call him John, so they would never slip up and it would become second nature for him to answer to that name. But now she was frightened, and Roberta had never feared anything. *This is ridiculous woman, pull yourself together.* She left her snoring lover and went into the hall. The moans could be made out quite clearly now, they sounded almost human. Roberta tried to walk with a confidence she did not feel as she approached the large oak staircase that led to the middle and upper levels of the house. Somehow, she knew that when she arrived on the first floor the sound would still be above her coming from the top floor. Since the day Harry had been confronted by his brother six months before they had neither talked about him nor ventured anywhere near the vault. The house was big enough without either of them having to face the scene of their horrendous crime.

Roberta stood at the bottom of the staircase on the second floor. The moaning had stopped but somehow, she had to face her fears and go up one more flight. Taking a deep breath, she placed her foot on the first step and instinctively lifted her head up. She did not need to take that next step because the eyes of her dead husband John were staring with venom down at her from the top of the landing. The figure was completely black, and pools of dripping liquid fell from it onto the carpet. It looked like a human who had fallen into a vat of tar but with increasing horror, Roberta realised it was parts of the decaying carcass falling away from the body. For a few seconds they looked at each other and then the apparition started to descend the stairs as it croaked out the words. 'Roberta, I love you. Why did you do it, why did you kill me?' But the object of its hatred and spite was already fleeing, screaming down the stairs for her accomplice Harry to save her.

When Harry had awoken later that evening to find the chalk white Roberta cowering in the corner of the living room he too was frightened. He had never seen the strong Roberta look this way, ever. He was convinced that she was hallucinating but the last thing he needed was her to start acting crazy. Over the next few days, he tried to help her while she lay shivering in the ground floor bedroom. He even considered calling in the village doctor but was glad when she insisted that it was too risky. Harry even dared to venture up to the third floor within sight of the vault, but all was silent and undisturbed. Within a few months' things had settled down again. Roberta kept a constant supply of mild sedatives and took them daily while Harry continued to drink more and more. Any thoughts of getting a housekeeper had disappeared and other than the occasional run to the shops the two Denham-Grangers kept themselves to themselves. The house continued to decline as Roberta lost interest in maintaining it and other than the weekly visit by the gardener things slowly started to crumble. Harry had even been forced to accompany Roberta on the six-monthly visits to see Mollet-Lambton and Harvie the estate solicitors. She would still do most of the talking but sometimes she would lose the thread and he would have to step in and make sure they were still receiving enough money to get by on.

One early spring morning in 1978 Harry found himself rummaging about on the second floor of Deadwater. It was not often he would even get up in the morning but lately, he had been making a real effort to stay off the demon drink. He had made the decision to try and get the house into some sort of order. He wanted to please Roberta, against all the odds he had grown quite fond of her. Maybe it was because she was all he had now. They no longer had a sexual relationship, but he would lay beside her at night as she would no longer sleep alone. As he searched through one of the old bedrooms Harry noticed a large bundle of newspapers piled up underneath a musty old bed. He pulled some of them out and looked at the date. *Christ 1957, the year the old man passed away. God, what I would not give to go back to then and be 29 again, working for the cartel and making a fortune.* Harry continued to clear out the rubbish from under the bed until he uncovered a small ornamental gold-plated chest. He dragged it out into the middle of the floor and was fascinated to see the name of his hated late father Leonard Denham-Granger imprinted on the lid. As expected, it was locked but he was intrigued to open it and see what was inside.

'Roberta, Roberta, come and see what I have found.' Within a few minutes, Roberta had appeared nervously at the bottom of the stairs. She had never fully recovered from the incident with the vision but tried her best to please Harry.

'What is it, what do you have?'

'It is some sort of treasure chest, it was under one of the beds in a back room. Come up and see if you recognise what it is while I go and get some tools to open it.' They passed each other on the landing as Harry raced excitedly down the stairs to get his hammer.

Roberta walked into the musty old room and spotted the ornate chest sitting in the middle of the floor. Somehow, she remembered it from her first years in the house with John. It had always had pride of place in old man Denham-Grangers downstairs office. No one had been allowed to touch it accept him. What was it doing hidden in this room? And then the memory kicked in. For some reason, Leonard had wanted to use one of the smaller upstairs bedrooms towards the end before he died. *This must have been the very room, yes, of course, that is why the chest was here.* He had kept it close to him even in his last days. She knelt beside it and ran her hands over the ornamental gold engravings before her fingers touched a hidden catch underneath the lid. Roberta flicked the little tab and pulled the lid of the cask open. Within seconds she was running to the top of the stairs with her arms full, a trail of dropped notes following in her excited footsteps.

'Harry, Harry in the name of heaven look, look.' Harry had already arrived at the bottom of the stairs even as Roberta's high-pitched voice screamed his name. 'Our troubles are over Harry, there must be thousands in the chest. This will be enough for us to keep running the house for a good few years at least.'

She was laughing hysterically with the release of

emotion that the extra money promised. Maybe it was not a fortune, but it would make a difference in helping to keep Deadwater going. But even as she threw the money into the air and hundreds of notes floated down towards her accomplice she was already sensing that something was not right. *Why was Harry looking up at her aghast with his mouth wide open in horror? He should be celebrating like me.* Roberta only had a split second to turn her head before she felt the full force of the brutal push and her feet buckled. Roberta's body crashed down the flight of stairs and rolled like a rag doll step by step towards Harry. Meanwhile, he stood transfixed like a rabbit in the headlights staring at the deathly shape of his dead brother looking down at him.

Over the next few years some of the money they had found helped to keep the two Denham-Grangers in food and coal for the fire. Once Harry had plucked up the courage to check the rest of the notes he had discovered many of them to be worthless. Junk that old Leonard had collected from various foreign business trips. They also had a meagre inheritance from the small amount that was left of the estate money. The reality was they spent very little, most of it went on booze for Harry. Roberta kept her aging yellow Cortina to buy supplies, mostly drink and of course, nothing was spent on the house, so it continued to look more run down every day. The gardener visited once a week but the most he could do was to keep the large lawns cut while the bushes and trees grew with abandon. Sometimes Harry would send the gardener to get his supply of booze and even the grass would not get done. Life became a matter of survival for the prematurely aging couple as they waited for the inevitable re-appearance of the vengeful ghost. They were trapped in Deadwater, they neither had the will nor the money to leave and dreaded someone finding the decaying remains of John Denham-Granger in the vault. All that was left was for Harry to drink himself into oblivion and for Roberta to keep herself doped up on sedatives to keep the fear in her soul at bay.

During 1980 that hopeless policeman had been spotted cycling up the drive on his bike. Luckily Harry was having a sober day and the two of them quickly put into action the plan they often talked about should they have visitors. After PC Chisholme left they congratulated each other on getting through it without raising any suspicion. But Harry was angry, he hated everyone in the village. Being stuck in the house and having little to do allowed his mind to wander and dream up conspiracy theories that did not exist.

A few months after the surprise visit by PC Chisholme Harry was having one of his very occasional walks into the village to restock his drink supply. Roberta hated him going in case it led to trouble but he insisted that they had to show some resemblance of normality. On arrival at The Oak, he downed a very quick four pints and then enquired of the barman why the main street was so quiet? Bill Tavey was taken aback as Denham-Granger rarely uttered a word other than to ask for a beer. In fact, the owner of the big house would usually only stay fifteen minutes and sit on his own in a corner. Today he had been in the pub for more than half an hour and was drinking very fast. 'It's the funeral of young Stephen Warton, tragic, he committed suicide. Most of the village are attending, I had to keep the bar or would be there myself.'

'Is that so. I shall go in and pay my respects then. Pour me another pint.'

Bill could tell the words were said with bitterness rather than with any respect for the dead boy. He was not sorry when Denham-Granger left shortly after having consumed another few pints. *Well, that is weird, he has changed so much from the early days. Probably that awful wife of his. God help them at the funeral if he turns up in that state.* Bill went back to washing the glasses in the empty pub as Denham-Granger slammed the door on his way out.

By the time Harry returned to Deadwater an hour later he was shocked to find Roberta cowering in the corner of the living room, tears streaking down her careworn face. More worryingly she was covered in bruises but would not talk about what had caused them. From that day on things went rapidly downhill for the lady of the house. Strangely the apparition never visited Harry again and would only torment Roberta until eventually, it became too much for her and she passed away in late 1983. In the latter years, Harry had taken to sleeping in the living room with his whisky bottle and would often be awoken by Roberta's screams. Again, he would find her alone, but her arms would be bruised as though she had been fighting someone off. The village doctor had been around a few times and Harry could tell he was being blamed for the injuries. Even that bastard Policeman Chisholme and his sidekick had called at the house and Harry had as always lost his temper and ended up fighting with them. They no longer had the yellow Cortina as he had written it off. So, now he was reduced to either walking to the village himself or paying the gardener to bring him back his drink supply. The death of Roberta was a release for them both. This was the kickstart he needed to get away from the curse of Deadwater for good.

Harry stepped out of the little police car. He was still laughing when he opened the front door into the crumbling mansion. *So that is what the fucking idiots all think. We killed our child and kept it hidden here, Jesus what a bunch of fucking low life morons. How the hell did they concoct that little tale up?* For the first time in years, Harry felt alive. Roberta's funeral had given him the push to make a new life for himself. Nine long years had passed since he had first come back, surely even the cartel had given up looking for him by now? He had talked it through with Mollet-Lambton the lawyer. Sell Deadwater for whatever he could get and then find a little place somewhere a long way from Witton Saint James. Maybe go to Spain, the demons of his past could surely not follow him that far. The sale would not make him rich, but he no longer cared. At least everything belonged to him now, *no other Denham-Grangers left to share it with.* He could retain his dead sibling's identity and that way he would always be safe. *Christ I am only 56, stop drinking now, get healthy, maybe even get me a new woman.* Yes, it all sounded perfect, but one last thing had to be done. Before Harry could even let the estate agents into price the large Deadwater estate he had one last act to do. Open the vault after eight years and bury the body of his brother somewhere it would never be found. And as you would expect, that was something the younger brother of the long-dead John Denham Granger was not looking forward to. Not looking forward to at all!

Thoughts:

I can remember when I was a child asking my parents if I could get the board games Cluedo or Mousetrap for Christmas. They would answer me with, *when I was a kid we used to be happy playing in the street with an old hoop and a stick.* Now when my kids ask for the latest smartphone or a Megabox Bluetooth Skyweaver Inkpad, I reply, *in my day we had to make do with playing board games and rolling a dice.* So, does that mean when our grandchildren ask for a city on Mars with full teleport channels our adult children will reply, *we had to survive with those old-fashioned smartphones when we were your age, but you know what? We were as happy as Larry.* Well, my real point is, Who the hell was Larry and why was he so happy? Was it because he had an old hoop and a stick to play with?

10

SO LONG, CRUEL WORLD

(Deadwater 1984)

Harry had a few weeks until his Lawyer Mollet-Lambton would arrive with the valuers. He decided to embrace his new chance in life and spend the time getting the crumbling house at least tidied up inside. He called Toby the gardener and offered him a generous sum to spend a full week trimming the trees and bushes in the large overgrown garden. Well, that was his plan, but *first things first thought* Harry. *Tomorrow I shall get that body upstairs sorted out, finally lay the demon to rest. You don't fucking scare me John, time to get you out of the house and into the ground. Can't have you spooking potential buyers now, can we?* He chuckled away to himself. Harry was in a good mood, the best mood he had been in for years. He was still laughing at the news that the villagers considered him as a child murderer. He emptied the bag he had carried back in the Police car and looked lovingly at the bottles of whisky. *All that stuff can wait until tomorrow Harry you fucking old genius, tonight is celebration time.* He yanked the top off the bottle and took a long swig before sitting down beside the unmade fire and letting the warm glow of the hard stuff consume his body instead.

Harry was well into the second bottle as he started to drift off to sleep. He could feel the chill envelop the large living room. He missed Roberta, even as she had succumbed to ill health she had still made up the fire and tried to look after him as best as she could. His hazy thoughts went back to the first six months after they had locked John in the vault. Things had been good, *why the hell did that pathetic brother of mine have to ruin it?* Sleep started to consume him, blurry images of his past life becoming mixed up in the pathways of his brain. Old Leonard, John, the cartel, Deadwater, the contract killings, Roberta, that village policeman, Witton Saint James, the vault, John, the vault, John, the....

Harry woke with a start. It was after two in the morning and he was freezing. *Time for bed old boy, just one last drink.* His eyes were still half shut as he reached for the bottle, the dim glow of the table lamp reflected the shadow of his arm as it searched for contact with the cold glass. And then he turned to look at the armchair that Roberta used to sit in opposite him. John seemed the same as he did the day they had locked him in the vault. He was smiling, dressed in his tweeds, the perfect country gentleman. Harry sat transfixed staring at the vision seated before him. 'What is it you want John? You are dead for God's sake, you are not going to drive me crazy the way you did with your old lady. It's fucking Harry here; do you know who you are messing with?' The apparition continued to look at him, that good-natured dim-witted grin he had always hated his brother for. The whispered reply came slowly as if the spectre was struggling to get the words out. The sound was sad almost pleading, the tone was the exact opposite of the smiling face.

'Harry, you need to help me. Please, God, help me, get me out of this half-life. In the name of Christ get me out of the vault, bury me properly. Release me from this torment.'

And then the vision started to change as Harry sat transfixed in mortal fear. John started to melt and decay until the stench of rotting dead flesh and bones became too overbearing for the younger brother. Harry snapped out of his trance and jumping quickly to his feet he fled out of the room. Within seconds he was standing outside on the porch of Deadwater. Even in the starlit night, the shadow of the house seemed to throw a blanket over him. But now Harry was determined, his brother had even told him what to do. Now was the time, he would do what he had been putting off for years. Open the vault and get rid of John once and for all.

Harry shone the torch around the shed searching for the tools he would need. He dragged the filthy tarpaulin out from under years of accumulated musty junk and carefully folded it over. He grabbed the spade and for some reason a large hammer and made his way to the back of the outhouse. Despite his advancing years and the bottles of whisky he had consumed Harry worked as a man possessed. He knew he had to get the job finished before daylight, just in case. Luckily the rain stayed away and soon even the cold had been replaced by sweat and exertion. By four in the morning, Harry had dug the trench. Tomorrow once daylight arrived he could work out a way to disguise the digging in case the gardener wondered what the newly turned earth was about.

Why the hell did I not grab the bottle before I left the room? Harry castigated himself as he stood admiring his handy work in the dim glow of the moon. Even though he longed for another drink he knew he could not face going back into the house unless it was to charge upstairs to the upper floor and do what he had to do. He placed the spade against the side of the outbuilding in readiness for his return. Taking one last deep breath Harry picked up the tarpaulin and the hammer before shining the torch towards the dark and imposing front of Deadwater House. This would have to be his only light. The former Tony Brendon was a professional killer, he would leave nothing to chance. Even the unlikely prospect of someone watching the building in the middle of the night had to be planned against. The house had to be kept in total darkness while he dragged the corpse downstairs into the newly dug grave.

Harry was not an easy man to intimidate, in fact, the harsh brutality of his past had hardened him to the point that nobody scared him. Whenever he had been cornered and it had become a matter of life or death then the younger Denham-Granger simply adopted a policy of my life and your death. But this was different, he was not sure if madness was causing the visions of his brother or he really was being haunted. Either way, he knew the solution lay in getting the body out of the vault and into the sanctuary of the earth. He crept slowly into the house. Even though the ghost had told him what to do, he somehow felt that it sounded all too easy. Something might try to stop him, *but just let them fucking try*. The hammer in his right hand was Harry's source of comfort, an implement to kill with. The blatant use of his fists or a more lethal weapon had always seen him survive no matter how bleak things might look. He took off his muddy jacket and hung it on the coat stand before making his way to the bottom of the stairs. Harry kept the beam of the torch focused on the top of the landing as he took each step. It was almost as if he expected to be challenged before he got to the vault. And then the familiar words of his father floated up through the darkness from the foot of the stairs that he had just left.

'Your mother is dead Harry, dead, when will you accept that and grow up.'

Harry turned and shone the torch down on the figure of his father below. Behind him stood a young-looking Roberta. The old man smiled at him, but his words sounded harsh. The way he had remembered them the day he had struck his father more than thirty years before.

'You leave this time and I swear to God Harry I am finished with you, no going back, no money, nothing. You walk out, and the door is shut forever, no inheritance, no allowance. I am damned if I will put up with your resentment any longer. You have threatened me one last time son, this time I mean it.'

But Harry was no longer listening. He was advancing back down the stairs, the hammer raised once again ready to kill the adversaries in front of him. The attack came from behind, he felt the hands on his throat before he had a chance to react. Strong powerful hands that gripped him and in one thunderous push slammed him hard against the wooden oak bannister. So hard that his neck broke and his body slid down to the lower floor. The decaying figure of John Denham-Granger stood hunched at the top of the stairs.

And finally, all was silent. The only sign of life left in Deadwater was the tortured breathing of the unconscious Harry and the torch that still shone. But soon even it would flicker and die.

***

(Witton Saint James 1984)

I remember the day it all ended as if it was yesterday. It was almost as though everything in my life before that moment had been leading up towards this pre-planned finale. I can even tell you the exact date because at the time I thought it was rather ironic that it was Saint Valentine's Day. Yes Tuesday, February 14th, 1984, go on check it up if you don't believe me. I am sure the library in Ludlow will have a file of old newspapers reporting the strange tale regarding the end of the Denham-Granger family. Faded yellow pages telling stories and mentioning names of long ago.

I was sitting in The Oak with Chris that afternoon feeling sorry for myself. Old Bill Tavey was pulling our first pint and as always, the pub gossip Farmer Davington was in his usual place at the bar. Even Doctor Chris Langton realised I was depressed that afternoon and was trying not to wind me up. It was the second day of my suspension and I had been given a date to report to the police headquarters the following week. It mattered not a jot because my resignation letter was already in my pocket, it just needed a stamp and off it would go. 'So young Chisholme, what will you do with yourself if you are not sleeping in the Witton police station or crashing cars?' The words from landlord Tavey were said without even a hint of sarcasm. I suppose by this point everyone in the village had sussed me out. I think they liked me because I turned a blind eye to the local drink driving but most knew I did very little real work.

'Not sure Bill if I am honest. My mother says I can move back with her while I sort things out. Maybe get a labouring job and go to evening classes. Maybe I will study to become a doctor like Chris here.'

Both Bill and Chris looked at each other and tried not to turn their barely disguised grins into fully fledged laughter. And then old Davington piped in with his tuppence worth.

'Can't even do the job of Policeman, don't knows how you be going to do the job of them, Doctors. You don't be clevur enough anyways, Chris ere be clevur but not you. Not by a long shot, no ways.' Bill Tavey chipped in quickly before Davington continued with his tirade.

'Why not go the whole way and become a brain

surgeon Gordon? But before you do young man, that will be £1.44.'

No doubt the polite mickey taking would have continued but suddenly Chris's pager started bleeping.

'Bloody hell, sorry Gordon I will need to call the surgery. They would not bleep me unless it was an emergency'

I shrugged, *just another thing to make me feel even worse*. I had fancied having an afternoon drinking session to drown my sorrows before posting the letter. Now even my reluctant drinking companion was going to abandon me. Within minutes Chris was back and went to grab his coat from the back of the bar stool.

'What is it? Another old biddy needing her emergency sleeping pills?' Chris was looking at me with a sense of excitement.

'Get your jacket Gordon, this might be your chance to lay some old ghosts to rest. The surgery had a call from the ambulance service. They are on the way to Deadwater House, it seems like the gardener has just found a badly injured John Denham-Granger laying on the floor.'

We turned into the familiar driveway of the old mansion. The trees and bushes lining the curve up to the Denham-Granger home had grown so much that they kept the panorama of the building hidden until you had almost arrived at the imposing front door.

The ambulance was already there but, in those days, they required a doctor on hand for serious emergencies. The front door of the house was open, it looked like it had been forced as the glass was smashed. I noticed Toby Bowman standing at the side of the steps. While Chris went inside to attend to the patient I stood at the entrance and tried to talk to the erstwhile Deadwater gardener. He had always been an odd bugger, most in the village talked about him having peculiar habits. He was shunned by the people of Witton Saint James, so it probably suited the Denham-Grangers to employ him. He was the sort of person who would not have looked out of place chewing a long piece of straw. 'Hi, Toby, what's happened here then?'

'Be none of your business then is it?' He spoke the words while looking down at the ground, almost as though I did not exist.

'Well, it might be Toby, considering I am a police officer. You have just found an injured man, so you really should try to answer my question.'

'Be not a policeman anymore though tis you from what I heard.'

'For fuck sake Toby, I am only asking you what's going on. I am not looking for a fucking confession.' At that point I was thinking to myself, *thank God I am going to get away from this nuthouse of a village, I have just had old Davington talking shite and now this fucking fruitcake.'*

'Still be none of your business Chisholme. Be sending up the real police from the big town if there be questions needing asked. Thems will send a tective not a constable cos you are not a tective.'

I could feel myself getting frustrated but tried to keep calm.

'Look, Toby, I am only asking because I am concerned for John Denham-Granger. I knew him quite well and had grown rather fond of him. Can you just tell me what you found when you broke into the house? It would be very helpful, and I would really appreciate it?'

Be lying thinks I Chisholme. Mr. Denham-Granger hated you from alls I could make out. Be not right you accusing me of breaking in either.

I was reaching boiling point but ploughed on in the hope the unhelpful bastard would offer me an olive branch. I tried to switch tactics and appeal to his ego instead.

'You really do a smashing job on the garden here Toby, I wish I had green fingers like you. Is Mr. Denham-Granger badly injured? I hope he is going to be ok.

'Be doctor's business if he be injured or not and garden be to do with me not you.'

My patience finally snapped.

'Oh, for fuck sake Toby, let's just forget I fucking asked shall we.'

And with that, the helpful Toby Bowman wondered off down the road leaving me wondering who the half-wit really was, him or me? I was starting to realise that some of the villagers just acted daft to keep me in my place. Ma Capley, Davington and now Toby. I wondered if they all got together in the evening to laugh at the dopey policeman who would never make it as a tective, I mean detective.

Chris came out to the porch to speak. Denham-Granger was conscious but paralysed. It seemed like he might have broken his neck in the fall, but they could not be sure of the full extent of his injuries until they got him to the hospital. It looked possible that he could have lain on the stair landing for almost two days until the gardener saw him and broke down the door. My friend looked at me, I think we both understood what had to be done. 'Gordon, I know you are not an acting policeman now. Can I leave you to call Ludlow police station from the house and wait until they get here? Someone will have to organise getting the place secure.'

'Yes, no problem Chris, get yourself to the hospital with Denham-Granger, I can always scrounge a lift back once the real police arrive.' Chris smiled in sympathy and then replied.

'Well if they send your friend Sergeant Bastard you

might end up having to walk.' We both laughed at the surreal circumstance that had taken over our supposed drinking afternoon. Chris came close to me so no one else in the bizarre gathering could hear him.

'Don't say I said it Gordon, but this is your chance. The rumours, the talk of haunting and dead children. Why don't you check the house out before you call Ludlow, see what you can find?'

The two ambulance men appeared, one at each end of the stretcher while Chris walked alongside trying to make the short walk to the van as painless as possible for the beleaguered Denham-Granger. I stood back as they shuffled past me, the patient wrapped in a grey blanket with his head just visible. But that was enough for his eyes to focus on me. 'Come to find the child have you Chisholme?' Even though he was paralysed the venom in his voice shot out like shards of glass.

'Finally going to get the chance for you and the rest of the scum in the village to have your day, eh Chisholme you fucking big creep.'

Even as they placed him in the back of the ambulance I could still hear his shouting and then he broke into an almost demonic laugh, each cackle laced with hatred and spite.

'A child eh Chisholme, hahahaha, a fucking child. Call yourself a policeman, you are a piece of garbage, a piece of fu....' The doors of the ambulance slammed shut, and I was spared anymore ranting from the clearly deranged very last Denham-Granger to leave Deadwater House.

I decided to explore the lower floor first. I felt like an intruder, searching through the lives of the dead and the dying. It became obvious that towards the end the last two occupants had lived in just a few rooms, almost as though the house had been slowly reclaiming each part of the building back. Ironically the tidiest parts of the mansion had been where the Denham-Grangers had long departed. Empty alcohol bottles littered the rooms they had used, old newspapers and clutter covered the floors. The house felt damp and unloved as paint peeled from the once ornate doors and window frames. Eventually, I found myself on the top floor standing outside what I thought was the room that Imelda had told me about. The very one I had attempted to investigate during my ill-fated climb to the upper window. The door looked as though it belonged in a bank vault and of course it was locked. I spent at least thirty frustrating minutes searching every cupboard and drawer for the missing key. Bunches of keys were ferried up and down the two flights of stairs, but nothing would fit the lock into the vault. Fucking Christ, *I might have known I would get this close and screw up.*

I cursed myself and everyone else I could blame as I walked to pick up the phone. My one and only chance to solve the mystery and once again fate was against me. 'Hello, Ludlow police station, how may I help?' But the phone was already back in its receiver before the woman at the other end had finished her sentence. I was staring at Denham-Grangers jacket hanging on the entrance hall coat stand. It was covered in mud and had obviously been placed there by its owner, probably on the same night he had plunged down the stairs. I knew straight away that the key was in the coat and it also looked as though Denham-Granger had been up to something in the garden outside.

I turned the key in the lock and slowly pushed the door open. The stench of dirt and decay hit me head on. At the time I was not to know that the room had been locked for eight years but it was not hard to imagine going by the smell. Old ledger books and papers had been scattered around the vault almost as though someone had been in a frenzy to find whatever it was they wanted. And then I saw it. The sight was so sad to look at, I could feel my eyes moisten with tears. Huddled up below the window were the pathetic remains of a human skeleton with a small bowl still grasped tightly in the bones of its fingers.

Sergeant Billy Raine did not seem so intimidating anymore. Maybe it was because I knew he no longer held any authority over me. To him, I was still just on suspension but the resignation letter in my pocket meant I now had the control over my own destiny. He seemed in a good mood, bouncing around the vault while forensic officers went about their business. I knew he was pleased because although I had discovered the body, the glory would reflect on him. 'Good work Chisholme, maybe we might make a policeman of you yet.' It was clear that the remains did not belong to a child but other than that the identity of the unfortunate person was unknown. A uniformed officer came running up the staircase.

'Sergeant, I think you had better come and see what we have found in the garden, sir.'

I followed Billy the Bastard out of the house feeling like a puppy following its master. We stood with the other constables and surveyed the trench that could only have been dug by Denham-Granger. In the house, a torch had been found still dimly lit along with a filthy old tarpaulin.

'You know what this means don't you Chisholme?'

I was desperate to reply, *Yes Sergeant Bastard, it means that John Denham-Granger was digging a tunnel to go and visit his relatives in Australia, Sir*, but of course, I didn't.

'Not sure Sir, what do you think yourself?'

Billy Raine took a long thoughtful breath as though he had suddenly become Columbo and then replied in a tone of clever authority,

'It means that John Denham-Granger was in the middle of trying to bury the body we found upstairs. We have him bang to rights Chisholme. I think we will give the Lord of Deadwater a few days to get his strength back and then pay him a visit. I will maybe ask you to come along as you seem to know him better than most.' I decided to wait until our visit to interview Denham-Granger before handing over my resignation letter. Somehow it felt as though I needed to see this whole thing out to the bitter end.

I was surprised to be left in the dark for nearly a week before Sergeant Raine knocked on the door of my cottage. He was alone, and it was clear from his demeanour that we would not be going anywhere. 'Well Chisholme, this has got to be the most bizarre thing I have ever been involved in during my long career.' I wanted to tell him just how weird the whole Deadwater story had been for the last eight years but decided he might think I was crazy.

'Unfortunately, Chisholme, I need to tell you that Denham-Granger passed away this morning, for some reason he could not talk, seems he damaged his throat in the fall. Either that or he used it as an excuse to keep quiet.' That did not fit in with the verbal assault he had inflicted on me while being stretchered out the week before.

'That's sad news Sergeant, even though I had many run-ins with John Denham-Granger I would not have wanted such a horrible end for him.'

'Ahh but that's the thing Chisholme, that's the thing.' Raine was doing his best Columbo impression again. 'The person in the hospital was not actually John-Denham-Granger.'

'What!!' This was not what I had expected to hear. Bastard really was starting to sound like Columbo now.

'No but that is not all Chisholme, that is not all. Get this, dental records show that John Denham-Granger was the body you found in the vault.'

'What the fuck…. that's impossible. I knew John, involved with him for years, how..what the fuck?' To say I was confused would be a massive understatement. 'So, who was the guy in the hospital then?'

'At the moment we are not sure until the results come back but, wait for this, it seems it might be his brother Harry Denham-Granger. From what we know he disappeared in 1950.'

Sergeant Raine picked up his coat to leave. The revelation had stunned me but somehow it made some sense. He looked at me and smiled. 'Maybe your suspension will be lifted soon Chisholme, you have certainly helped your cause by bringing this strange affair to light. I might even forgive you for wrecking one of my police cars.'

He went to open the door and then turned to face

me.

'Well that's two odd things, they say good news comes in three's, I hope not as I have had enough of all this for now Chisholme. His tone sounded sarcastic without being mean.

'Oh Sergeant, I almost forgot, I have something I need to give to you.'

I reached into my pocket and handed him the letter. He looked at me wearily and placed it inside his coat.

'Yes, I think I know what this is Chisholme. Maybe the best thing for everyone, in the long run, a fresh start eh?' He placed his hand on my shoulder before disappearing out of the door for good.

'I hope things work out for you Gordon. Look after yourself young man.'

The following morning, I packed my bags and with the help of my mate Chris Langton I squeezed my entire belongings into the hire car. 28 years old and my whole life held in a suitcase and some plastic bags. 'Keep in touch Gordon, life in the village will not be the same without you. You had better come back in a few months as promised and buy me that farewell drink.'

'Yes, I will Chris, of course, I will. You just try and stop me.' I did not realise at the time that I was lying. It would be another 26 years before I would return in

2010. Maybe my real journey into adulthood started that day after all.

There was one last thing to do before I closed the chapter on my life that involved Deadwater, Imelda Poole, The Denham-Grangers and Witton Saint James. I pulled the car into an empty space at Ludlow hospital and went to find Ward 3A, the last resting place of the man I knew as John Denham-Granger. Don't ask me why but somehow it felt wrong not to attend his funeral, so this just seemed to be the best way of finishing things. Pay my respects and then disappear. I sat outside the ward drinking tea from a plastic cup while my mind played over the last eight years. Maybe it was Imelda or the dream of Imelda that I was really saying goodbye to. The vision of her long curls and blue shining eyes in my head was suddenly interrupted by a hospital porter pushing a trolley. 'You looking for someone mate, are you the press?'

'No, I just came up to pay my respects to the recently departed, what makes you ask anyway?'

He stopped pushing the empty trolley and gave me a sympathetic smile. 'Sorry mate, it's just that we have been overrun by the tabloids in the last couple of days after they brought that posh guy up from Witton Saint James. Police all over the place as well.'

My eyes lit up as I sensed the chance to grab the information I was looking for. 'Yes, that's him, that's why I am here. I knew him, it was me who found the body, well one of the bodies. Did you hear how he died, was it the shock of the fall he had?'

The friendly porter walked over and sat down in the empty seat beside mine and introduced himself as Ben. I could tell he was enjoying the opportunity to tell his tale again. Anyway, have you ever known a hospital porter who did not grasp the chance to sit down?

'Well, that's the strange thing. I heard that he crushed his throat when he fell, and he lay unable to move for a couple of days. When they brought him in here he was very weak through lack of food and water but, he was still able to talk. Seems like he went rapidly downhill once he got here. They could not understand why. Some said he had lost the will to live, as though he was frightened to pull through.'

'So, what happened to him then, what was the cause of his death given as?'

My confidant moved his head closer to me and in a low whisper replied, 'They tell me he died of dehydration, no matter what they did he could not keep anything down, plus he was very weak anyway. It was a real shame.'

I stood up having heard all I wanted to know. So, Harry had suffered almost the same death he had inflicted on his brother by all accounts. 'Well thanks for the information, I had better be on my way.'

'Are you related to the guy who died then, a family member?' Ben clearly did not relish the prospect of having to get back to work as he tried to continue the conversation.

'No, I was, let's just say we knew each other.'

Ben stretched his arms out and gave a yawn before walking over to take his position up behind the trolley again. Just as he was about to head off he turned to me and gave his parting shot. 'Shame he died like that. I felt sorry for his brother, well I assumed it was his brother, certainly looked the image of the guy in the bed. He came up and sat outside his room each evening, never said a word or even went into the ward. Just sat there staring at him.' Ben's words grabbed my attention immediately.

'His brother? That's odd, did you get a chance to speak to him yourself?'

'No, to be honest, I thought he was a bit weird, I would say hello when I passed but he would just ignore me and keep his eyes on that Denham-Granger chap.' I sighed and stood up to head back to my car and hopefully forget about all this.

'I take it after Denham-Granger died then the guy, I mean his brother disappeared?'

Ben reluctantly started to push the trolley away from me as though the thought of having to work again was unbearable.

217

'You could speak to him yourself. Don't ask me why but he is sitting outside on the bench near The Memorial Garden. God knows why he is back?' I started to run before it suddenly dawned on me I had no idea where I was going. Ben had almost disappeared around the corner of the corridor.

'Ben, Ben, how do I get to The Memorial Garden?'

Luckily the hard-working porter had stopped to chat with someone else.

'Follow the signs for Ward 5B, take a left at the café and then turn right at the Oncology Department, head straight on and you can't miss it, It's just next to the Porters office.'

'Within minutes I was lost. *For fuck sake, Gordon slow down and listen to the instructions the next time you ask.* I spotted a knowledgeable looking medical person sporting a gleaming white coat.

'Excuse me, I need to find the Porters office, any idea which way?

The coat eyed me up and down as though I had asked for ten pence for a cup of tea and a cigarette.

'Go down to the end of this corridor and then turn right at the café, follow the signs for the Cardiology Department and then head past ward 4D, the porter's office is just along from that, you can't miss it.'

Very quickly I was lost again but by some good fortune, I finally arrived at the Porters Office. The little garden stood opposite surrounded by glass. And there he was sitting with his back to me on a bench, alone except for the trees and flowers. I searched desperately for a way out to see him, but the door was on the opposite side of the garden and no way was I going to ask for fucking directions again. If I am honest I was knackered with all the running, maybe it was time to stop smoking as well. I edged up close to the large glass frame and rattled my hand against it. Slowly the figure stood up and turned around to face me. It was him, John Denham-Granger but not the one I had grown to hate. It was the kind well-dressed dapper gentleman I had first met in 1975. He smiled and started to walk towards me….Fucking hell, someone had grabbed my shoulder.

'That's a shame, I take it you missed him then? I looked at Ben the porter in shock for a few seconds before turning back to look through the glass.

'No, No, he is there look……' but, the garden was empty.

For the first time in years, I felt contented. The curse was over, all the Denham-Grangers were gone. Deadwater no longer held us in its icy grip. The new dawn had arrived for me and the villagers of Witton Saint James. I just wished that Imelda had been with me to witness it as well.

Thoughts:

I always wished that I could live life in reverse. How amazing it would be to be born old and worldly wise and then grow younger each day. My aches and pains would get better rather than worse. I would know the regrets that are coming and be able to head them off at the pass. Imagine being able to tell the person who had died that you loved them. Of course, like everything in life, it would have its downside. You could be enjoying a nice beer in the pub and the barman would come over and say, *sorry son you need to leave, you just turned 17.*

11

THE MANSION OF FORGOTTEN DREAMS

(The B 7027 to Witton Saint James 2010)

I had been dreading driving through Ludlow and finding it completely changed but it turned out to be a pleasant surprise. The house that bordered the River Teme still stood, added to since I had been a child but at least it was still there. In the intervening 26 years, more roads and a lot more houses had appeared, but it was still basically the same place.

I had barely stayed a matter of months with my mum after leaving Witton Saint James in 1984 as she was driving me crazy. To be fair I think I was having the same impact on her as well. It was around about that time that she met Jack, he was ok, but the fact was he would never replace my father. When my mum told me that he would be moving in I knew I had to get out fast. It's strange how life can change so much based on one little decision. I jumped into the first job that came up and by 1985 I was living in Glasgow. I had never even been to Scotland before but since then it has been my home. I even managed to carve out a successful career away from the police force, I bet you did not expect that? Ok maybe I never made it as a brain surgeon but trust me, working in the finance industry turned out to be quite lucrative. I could just imagine the stunned faces of old Davington or Landlord Bill Tavey if they had lived long enough to hear that Dopey big Gordon had become a stockbroker.

The old PC Chisholme still lived on though in my failed relationships. The longest anyone had been able to put up with me was eleven years, that was Evi. To be fair to me though, we would have still been together had cancer not so cruelly intervened in 1998. She was the love of my life, a perfect match, it was a shame we could not have children, it would have been a perfect legacy. After Evi died I never really held down a relationship for more than six months at best.

My mother had remarried and moved away not long after I had left so there had never been any reason to come back. The only contact I had with Witton Saint James was my old friend Doctor Chris Langton. It amazed me he had stayed in the village all his life, just like his father. I had met him on a good few occasions over the intervening years, but it had always been in Glasgow. Chris loved his football, I could take it or leave it. For a country doctor living in a Shropshire village on the Welsh border, it always seemed odd to me that he supported one of the famous Glasgow teams. It was his main passion in life other than his job and family. Even his two boys had developed an affinity with the city and they would come up and either stay with me or other friends he had. I bet you are wondering which team? Sorry, I can't tell you that, if you lived in Glasgow like me you would understand why.

I finally found my way onto the B7027 and the road to my erstwhile haunting ground if you will pardon the pun. Even the name Witton Saint James on the road sign stirred up mixed emotions in me. I had finally succumbed to Chris's pleading to come and stay for a few days with him in the village. It was not that he was desperate for me to return, I think he just felt obliged to reciprocate the fact that I had put him up at my house in Glasgow so often. Two days, that would be all, I was just not comfortable staying in a house with a couple and their two sons. Don't get me wrong, I liked Samantha his partner, but it just felt invasive staying there. I know what it really was, it was being single. If I had Evi with me I would not have felt like such an outsider. Being in your fifties and single has a certain stigma. It was as though people either had me down as gay but not willing to admit it or a trainspotter and still not willing to admit it. OK, maybe it was just me being paranoid. That's the other thing about living on your own, you get far too much time to think.

I deliberately avoided the road that went past Deadwater House although I did intend to visit before I left. My plan was to go up to see the old Mansion on the way back to Glasgow. That would be my final act as I fully intended never to come back. To be perfectly honest I was already regretting my decision to allow Chris to finally convince me to make this visit, too many bad memories, too many forgotten dreams.

Witton Saint James looked different. Not that it had grown much, just a few houses added here and there. No, it looked far more affluent then I remembered it. Everywhere seemed well kept, neatly manicured gardens, Monoblock driveways, and modern house extensions. Large 4x4 cars parked outside nearly every building. In fact, the amount of traffic seemed to have the little village in gridlock, I would not have lasted a week if it had been as busy as this when I was the village Bobbie. Chris had warned me about the changes. The village was no longer a place you grew up in and knew everybody's business. As the older generation had died out the houses had been sold to outsiders, commuters who stayed in Witton Saint James rather than lived in it. It was as though someone had lifted a section of middle-class suburbia and placed it neatly on top of the village I used to know. The little police station was long gone, replaced by a modern bungalow. Stokely's garage was still standing although now it had a handsome wooden sign displaying its new status, *Witton Saint James World Famous Antique Emporium.* It was comforting to see The Oak still looked pretty much the same, at least from the outside. Even the repair to the car park wall that Denham-Granger had demolished still stood out as a reminder of the bad old days.

I stood at the edge of the little garden and surveyed the tiny cottage I had once lived in. The very one where I and Imelda had laughed the evening away nearly thirty years ago. How things can change. It was now a large bungalow although the basic shape of the original building remained. I was desperate to knock on the door and ask if it still had an outside toilet but decided they might call the police. Just my luck if old Sergeant Bastards son arrived and tasered me to the ground before slapping on the cuffs.

The first night I stayed in Chris's beautiful large house Samantha made dinner while I and my old buddy reminisced and got very drunk. We talked about the old faces, Paul Davington, Ma Capley and the Denham-Grangers. Now that I was back in the village I was desperate to ask if Chris knew anything about Imelda Poole. I had always avoided mentioning her when he had visited Scotland in case it sounded like I still had an immature crush on her. *I will ask him tomorrow when I sober up,* I thought to myself.

The following morning, we stood beside the graves of the Denham-Grangers at Saint John's on The Mound church. It's odd how things can take on a different perspective when you have not seen them for so long. The main church building seemed so much smaller than how I remembered it. Even the gate I had stood beside to welcome the mourners attending Steven Wharton's funeral looked as though it had shrunk. The very place I had watched Imelda walk through with her family all those years ago. She seemed so much like an immature dream now, I felt embarrassed even thinking about her and my crush. The eerie silence was broken by Chris, 'It's strange to see the graves all lined up so close to each other, after what happened.' I looked at each in turn as the long grass shuffled in the breeze around each headstone.

Mary Denham-Granger Born August 17th, 1900, Died September 11th, 1940

Leonard Denham-Granger Born June 12th, 1880, Died February 17th, 1957

John Denham-Granger Born September 2nd, 1924, Died June 8th, 1976

Roberta Denham-Granger Born November 11th, 1926, Died December 17th, 1983

Harry Denham-Granger Born May 23rd, 1928, Died February 16th, 1984

'Yes Chris, you are right, it does seem odd. Somehow I can imagine them all still fighting over the Denham-Granger money even though they are under the ground.' Chris chuckled before returning the conversation back to a melancholier tone.'

'I never thought about it before, but the two boys were only relatively young when Mary died, Christ, she was only 40 herself. Maybe things would have turned out differently if she had stayed around.'

'Yes, but somehow I doubt Mary and Roberta would have seen eye to eye. That Roberta was a scary woman, well at least she was when I first met her. I liked John though, well the real John not his brother the imposter. Harry was a total nut job. It was strange that the whole thing was sort of hushed up. I hardly read anything about it after I left.'

Chris shrugged and turned to walk away. 'Well, that's the thing about the upper class in those days. There was no reason to prosecute anyone as they were all dead when the truth came out. It was sort of hushed up, no one in the village wanted that stain against the name of Witton Saint James. Everything just clammed up and the whole affair was rarely mentioned.

'And Deadwater House, what happened to it over the years?

'Well just like the Denham-Granger name, it faded away. They tried to sell it, but no one wanted a house that big, times had changed. Initially, the rooms were let out to students and farm workers but with no money spent it started to fall into decay. Then after years of protracted wrangling, it was purchased by property developers with a plan to turn it into luxury apartments and then, well you will see it tomorrow on your way home.' As Chris was talking the memory of the close call with Malachy Proctor the grave digger came to mind. Don't ask me why but it did.

'I got propositioned by an old man at this graveyard once.' Chris was already laughing as he replied.

'Well, at least you can say you had some success then. From what I remember every girl you went out with in Witton turned into a disaster.' I ignored his mickey taking and continued my reminiscing.

'Yes, I am sure his name was something like, Michael Proctor, no hang on, Malachy Proctor. That was his name. He kept touching me up, had a face that only a mother could love.' Chris was now laughing his head off.

'Malachy Proctor, Christ everyone knew to keep away from him Gordon. He was a serial man chaser, he tried it on with every young guy in the village, not just you.'

'Fuck, thanks, Chris. The memory of my one successful Witton Saint James relationship and you go and ruin it for me.' We strolled back to the car while still chuckling about the old days.

'Time for a beer Gordon, and it's your round first.'

The interior of The Oak had changed beyond recognition. It was now a posh restaurant although it still retained a bar selling a multitude of lagers and beers. Old Bill Tavey the long-dead landlord would have been turning in his grave at the thought of his customers asking for anything more than a pint and change for the cigarette machine. The fact was it now had more woman and children in it than you would have seen in a whole year in my time as the village policeman. The old bar cronies of the day came to the pub to get away from women, not to meet up with them.

I sipped my lager while feeling utterly self-conscious. It was not Chris's fault, the fact that he was the village doctor meant he knew everyone and they all wanted to say hello or talk about their dodgy knee operation. A few times Chris tried to politely introduce me as the ex Witton policeman but most just nodded a quick hello before focusing back on the village celebrity. And then suddenly I felt a poke in the back. I turned around, I knew the face, but the name would not come. 'PC Gordon Chisholme, how the hell are you?' He went to shake my hand but could see the confusion in my eyes.

'It's Robbie, Robbie Taylor. You must remember me, you gave me and my friends a bit of a time when we were kids.'

'Bloody hell, Robbie Taylor. Of course, I remember you, it's just been such a long time. You used to hang about with Carl, Steven and what was her name, oh yes I almost forgot, Imelda, Imelda Poole.' I was sure I could feel Chris smirking beside me at my pretence I had forgotten her name.

Robbie's expression changed slightly. 'Yes, it was such a shame about Steven and Carl, anyway, it was a long time ago.'

'So, Robbie, when did you move back to the village. I assumed you had left for good?' Robbie smiled and turned to show the large lady and three teenagers standing impatiently behind him waiting to leave.

'I came back in the early nineties Gordon, met my partner Michelle here and these are my three boys. You must remember Michelle, Michelle Poole, she was Imelda's sister.'

It was one of those awkward moments you occasionally have in life where neither party wants to be there, but you must finish the act so as not to upset everyone else involved. Michelle was the girl who had ditched me because I kept mentioning her sister every time we went on a date. She gave me a cursory smile, 'Hello Gordon, nice to see you again, I hope you are keeping well.' It was obvious she still remembered being compared to her sibling all those years ago. That old saying about a woman scorned came to mind.

'Right, we need to go now Robbie, I will catch you outside.' She walked off with the kids following while Robbie went to grab my hand for one last farewell shake.

'Great to see you again Gordon, will you be here for long?'

'No, I am heading home tomorrow Robbie, back to Glasgow, just popped out to see what The Oak was like nowadays. To be honest so much has changed, other than Chris you are the first person I have recognised.'

'Yes, it has changed a lot even in the last ten years Gordon, mostly newcomers. It's a coincidence but we have another visitor from Scotland staying at ours for a few days. Imelda my sister in law is down from Edinburgh, you must remember her, why don't you pop over and say hello?'

'No, its ok Robbie, I will be heading away early tomorrow, tell Imelda I was asking about her though.' Robbie gave one last grin and turned to walk away.

'Well if you do want to say hi to her Gordon, just wave because Imelda Is sitting over in the far corner. She is out for dinner with one of her old friends as well.' And with that, he was gone.

I spent the next thirty minutes trying to pretend to

Chris that I was not looking through the sea of diners to the table Imelda was sat at. It looked like her, but it was difficult to make out for certain as she had her back to the bar we were seated at on the other side of the large lounge. Chris winked at me, 'Imelda Poole eh, well who would have thought it, her being back for a visit at the same time as her number one fan club Gordon Chisholme. I am surprised you are not already over at her table with your tongue hanging out asking for her autograph.'

He continued to rib me, even mimicking my pretence to Robbie that I had forgotten her name. 'Ooh, what was her name again Robbie? What was that you said, oh yes, I remember her now, she had completely slipped my memory.' Chris said all this in a high-pitched squeaky voice just to push the joke home.

The beer was flowing and for the first time since arriving back at Witton Saint James, I started to relax and enjoy myself. This feeling lasted exactly another thirty minutes before things changed. Chris piped up, 'Right Gordon old boy, it's your round, we better make this the last one as I promised Samantha we would be back by nine.' I looked at my watch,

'It's only eight, Jesus Chris you are going soft. We can get at least another four in before then.'

But Chris was looking straight through me at the person approaching the bar.

'Doctor Chris Langton and PC Gordon Chisholme, well I never. What brings you two old timers out to party then?' Imelda Poole still looked amazing for 48. Ok like everyone she had aged, and some lines crossed her face, her dark curls now replaced by shorter blonde hair. She was dressed immaculately and still looked slim and sophisticated. Suddenly I was in my twenties again, back in love and feeling like a fool. Imelda smiled at me, those same expressive blue eyes and the well-honed ability to make me feel totally inadequate.

'Lost for words Gordon? Some things never change.' She still had that knack of being cheeky without it sounding rude.

'Hi, Imelda, what brings you to Witton?' I know it is wrong to admit it, but my eyes perked up at her reply.

'Oh, I am just down for a rare visit to see Michelle, she is the only one who still lives locally. I live near Edinburgh. It is home for me now, I have been there so long.'

'That's amazing, you are not so far away from me, I live in Glasgow, have for years. And how is...? Her face looked sad as she replied.

'Oh, Claudio passed away a few years back. I still miss him so much, but life goes on.'

'Sorry to hear that Imelda, I really am. I lost my

partner some years ago as well, so I know how you must feel.'

'Oh dear, that is awful Gordon. It is strange the way life can turn in just a moment.' She was giving me her full concentration now, Chris for the first time in the evening was being ignored. I scrambled about trying desperately to think of something clever to say.

'Well if you are ever in Glasgow you should pop in and say hello. I am not that far away from you in Edinburgh,' was sadly the best thing I could come up with. We looked at each other for a what seemed like an eternity. Each of us waiting for the other to say something, make the connection but even in my fifties, I was still a hopeless case when confronted by Imelda Poole. She gave that resigned smile I had seen her do so many times before and started to turn towards the door.

'Oh, one last thing Gordon. I never did get the chance to thank you.'

'Thank me for what Imelda?'

'Well, I don't know exactly what you did but thank you anyway, The Deadwater thing, you know. I heard you found the body. Everything has been fine since then. You promised you would look after me and you did. I will always remember you for that.' And then with a last goodbye, she put on her coat and walked out of the door. Chris gave me a look that said it all.

'Bloody hell Gordon, that was your one chance, you could have asked for her number at least? What the hell was there to lose? It was obvious that she wanted you to say something, and all you could do was go red and stammer like a kid. You are the same as you were in your twenties, you big idiot.' But even before he had finished the words I was off my chair and running to the exit.

'Imelda, Imelda, wait just a minute please.' She turned around with first a look of surprise on her face and then relaxed.

'Yes Gordon, what is it?'

'I just wondered, well look I am going to visit Deadwater House tomorrow, I just thought...well wondered if you fancied one last look around, for old time sake before we head away back to our real lives.' She threw her head back and laughed, I knew an Imelda answer was coming.

'Ok PC Chisholme, how about ten o'clock in the morning? You bring the joints and the whisky this time though.' She winked at me and walked off into the darkness of the evening.

Thoughts:

If someone asked you how many times you have been in love, would you really be able to answer the question? I am not sure that being in love really exists, maybe it gets confused with lust and sex. But no matter who you are with, the passion bit eventually dies and something long term must replace it. I think you are truly in love when the realisation comes that you have a soulmate. Sometimes it takes years but eventually, you know that life without that person would not be life. So, if someone stopped me in the street and said, how many times have you been in love? My answer would be, oh loads of times but I have only one soulmate.

12

LOVERS LANE

(Deadwater House 2010)

Old habits die hard, I nearly mangled another car on the road outside Deadwater. Chris had told me the place was now a construction site, but I still expected to be able to take the car up the private driveway to the edge of the house. No such luck, the tall mesh fencing blocked the path and the car brakes saved me by inches from ploughing into it. I suppose I was lost in my thoughts, you probably have an idea why by now if you have been paying attention. At least if I had smashed the car up it would have been mine to write off this time. Small mercies as they say.

I reversed back onto the B Road and parked up alongside a hedge, hopefully leaving enough room for the construction traffic that was bobbing back and forth along the road. A large billboard displayed a picture of two-story villas and neatly laid out flats with a smiling young couple holding hands outside one of them. I assumed they must have won the lottery because you could tell these buildings would not be cheap. The new development was called Blue Water Estates, obviously the name Deadwater would have been too much for the prospective buyers to handle. It always annoyed me how every new middle-class housing estate would have a twee name like Serendipity Mews or Everglade Dell. You could imagine the estate agents calling up. 'We have the perfect house for you Mr. Chisholme, it is in Rose Bloom Glade.'

'Oh, that sounds positively lovely. Do you have the address, so I can go and look at it?'

'Yes, it's, 24B Rose Bloom Glade, Chernobyl, Ukraine.'

It was just after 10 in the morning as I squeezed through the mesh fencing and started to walk up the familiar drive of the old mansion. The trees and bushes had been drastically cut back, no doubt in preparation for their removal later. I reached the top of the track and there it was in all its faded glory. Unlike the church back in Witton Saint James, the house still looked as large as I had remembered it. But now it was forlorn, every window was smashed, and ugly boarding surrounded the lower floor. 'Sorry mate, this is a restricted area, you can't stay here.' The guy with the hard hat looked like the officious type, you could tell his name was Health and Safety just by looking at him.

'Ok sorry mate, I was just hoping to have a last look. I used to know the occupants many years ago.'

'Well the occupants are long dead sir and you might end up with them if you hang around here any longer. Too much construction traffic uses this road, I really must ask you to leave.'

'Could I just wait on the side of the driveway then? I am expecting to meet someone.'

'Sorry sir, you will need to go back to the B Road, this is private property and a dangerous area for the public.' It felt like I was back talking to Toby Bowman the unhelpful gardener only this time he had found half a brain to use. But Health and Safety man was all heart really. 'I tell you what sir, if you want a safe view but just as close, you can drive around to the car park at Deadwater wood, it looks onto the back of the house and is a public path.

I walked dejectedly back to my car, not because the visit to Deadwater was over but more because it was now nearly 10.30 and Imelda had not turned up. I suppose I was not too surprised, she had made a good job of dodging me all my life. *Probably already on the way back to Edinburgh by now thanking her lucky stars that she had escaped without having to meet that awkward ex Policeman again.* I sat for another twenty minutes and watched the depressing site of countless dumper trucks and diggers rolling up and down the road towards the old mansion. *Time to finally lay the ghosts to rest Gordon and get back to your real life.* I started up the car and headed out on the B Road towards Ludlow and my long journey home to Glasgow. And yet for some reason, I had hardly gone a mile before I stopped and reversed up a farm track to go back the way I had come. Within seconds I was heading towards Witton Saint James, taking the road to the little wood at the back of Deadwater. It felt like John Denham-Granger was not letting go of me to go just yet.

It was now after eleven and I was desperate to get on the road and make it home before dark. Maybe even meet the boys and have a beer to celebrate a part of my life that was disappearing forever. I parked the car next to a red convertible already sitting in the little car park of Deadwater wood and made my way through the trees. She was standing there with her hands in her coat pockets and her hood pulled up as protection from the chill wind that blew towards the big house. Her back faced me as she concentrated on the decaying mansion. Imelda turned around and smiled. 'I thought you said ten o'clock? It's after eleven and I am bloody freezing Chisholme.'

'I was here at ten, up at the front of the house. I just assumed you had stood me up again.' She pulled the hood down and ruffled her hair while laughing.

'God Gordon, that is so you. Everyone knows you

meet in the woods to spy on Deadwater, the Denham-Grangers would never allow the likes of us to walk up their Driveway.'

We stood side by side and surveyed the crumbling ruin of our youth. Already the demolition team had removed most of the slates and other salvageable parts of the house before the rest would be confined to dust. Much of the once loved lawns and gardens had been flattened to allow foundations to be dug for the new houses. Lorries plied back and forwards churning the ancient greenery into pools of oozing mud. Soon it would all be gone and the last memories of the Deadwater ghost would die with it. I looked up at the window, the one that had cursed us all. I was sure I could see someone looking out although at that distance it was difficult. It gets hard at my age when your sight is not as good as it used to be. 'Do you see someone in the little window Imelda?' She ignored my question and turned to face me.

And then Imelda Poole did the exact opposite of what I expected her to do. You see that's why I loved her so much, have I mentioned that before? She placed her hand in mine and let those smiling blue eyes burn deep into my heart before replying.

'Do you know that when I was young we used to call this path Lovers lane?'

And then we walked hand in hand with our backs to Deadwater House accompanied by the sound of falling bricks and splintering wood as the demolition team got to the real work.

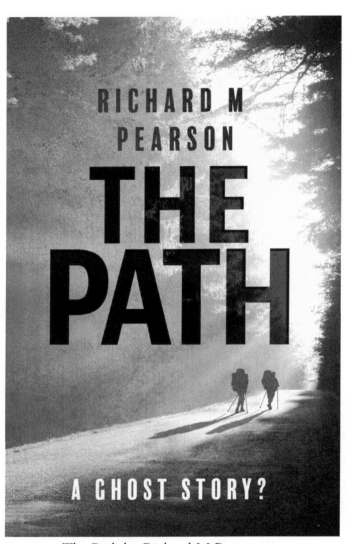

RICHARD M
PEARSON

THE
PATH

A GHOST STORY?

The Path by Richard M Pearson

On a path filled with ghosts and secrets, nobody is safe.

For neurotic Ralph and easy-going Harvey, the trek across the remote, rolling hills of Scotland is a chance to get away from life, an opportunity to rediscover their place in the world. At least that's the plan. But they are two middle-aged, unfit men trying to cross one hundred miles of rugged terrain.

Despite that, they might have had a chance if that was their only problem. Unfortunately, not only are they alcoholics, someone or something is stalking them, watching their every move. Worse, one man carries a terrible secret about why he went on the trip. A secret that will turn a friendly trek into something far darker. It's a safe bet that if either man survives, he will never be the same again.

***

The Path is the first novel by Richard M Pearson. A gothic ghost story for modern times that builds up an atmosphere of foreboding and fear.

A terrific read. Thoroughly enjoyed this novel. Atmospheric, melancholic, laced with pathos and wry humour. Excellent plot and an intriguing outcome. Strong characterisation, complex and endearing personas, more so for their flaws and imperfections. The poems were also a nice touch. Almost offering a staging post for the author's state of mind as each chapter ends. I can highly recommend The Path, it won't disappoint.

(Available on Amazon)

Made in the USA
Columbia, SC
15 August 2020

16455423R00148